"You're The One Who Has Amnesia," Tyler Muttered. "Why Am I The One Who Can't Seem To Remember His Own Name?"

Jenny smiled up at him. "Maybe my problem is contagious. Have you ever thought of that?"

"Maybe *you're* contagious."

"Poor Sheriff Cook. Saddled with contagious me. And I know how much you want to get rid of me."

She stared at the cleft in his stubborn chin. Up to his lashes, which were indecently long for a man and curled at the tips. His lips were also in her line of vision, and she couldn't help remembering what they had felt like on hers. *Cowboy*, she thought. *Rugged, tough...sweet...*

Without thinking, she kissed him again.

He stood frozen in the doorway, looking down at her with comical disbelief. "What was that for?"

She smiled innocently. "I have no idea. Maybe *you're* contagious...."

Dear Reader,

Welcome to Silhouette Desire! This month we've created a brand-new lineup of passionate, powerful and provocative love stories just for you.

Begin your reading enjoyment with *Ride the Thunder* by Lindsay McKenna, the September MAN OF THE MONTH and the second book in this beloved author's cross-line series, MORGAN'S MERCENARIES: ULTIMATE RESCUE. An amnesiac husband recovers his memory and returns to his wife and child in *The Secret Baby Bond* by Cindy Gerard, the ninth title in our compelling DYNASTIES: THE CONNELLYS continuity series.

Watch a feisty beauty fall for a wealthy lawman in *The Sheriff & the Amnesiac* by Ryanne Corey. Then meet the next generation of MacAllisters in *Plain Jane MacAllister* by Joan Elliott Pickart, the newest title in THE BABY BET: MACALLISTER'S GIFTS.

A night of passion leads to a marriage of convenience between a gutsy heiress and a macho rodeo cowboy in *Expecting Brand's Baby*, by debut Desire author Emilie Rose. And in Katherine Garbera's new title, *The Tycoon's Lady* falls off the stage into his arms at a bachelorette auction, as part of our popular BRIDAL BID theme promotion.

Savor all six of these sensational new romances from Silhouette Desire today.

Enjoy!

Joan Marlow Golan

Joan Marlow Golan
Senior Editor, Silhouette Desire

Please address questions and book requests to:
Silhouette Reader Service
U.S.: 3010 Walden Ave., P.O. Box 1325, Buffalo, NY 14269
Canadian: P.O. Box 609, Fort Erie, Ont. L2A 5X3

The Sheriff &
the Amnesiac

RYANNE COREY

Published by Silhouette Books
America's Publisher of Contemporary Romance

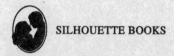

SILHOUETTE BOOKS

ISBN 0-373-76461-8

THE SHERIFF & THE AMNESIAC

Visit Silhouette at www.eHarlequin.com

Printed in U.S.A.

RYANNE COREY

is the award-winning author of over twenty romance novels. She is also the recipient of the *Romantic Times* Lifetime Achievement Award. She finds the peace and beauty of the mountains very conducive to writing, and currently lives in the beautiful Rocky Mountains of Utah. She has long believed in the healing power of love and laughter, and enjoys nothing more than bringing a smile to a reader's face.

You can write to her at 520 C. North Main, Suite 321, Heber City, Utah, 84032.

One

Jenny Kyle was getting a headache. This particular headache began with a capital "T," as in *trapped*. Quite simply, she couldn't stand being constrained in any way, shape or form. Especially when it wasn't her fault.

At least she was an optimistic claustrophobic. As soon as she had everything sorted out with the strong arm of the law, she would leave this unfriendly town of Bridal Veil Falls—Bride Falls on Her Head was more like it, she thought wryly—in the dust. Her headache would be only a memory. One SOS call to good old Lawyer Dearbourne would solve everything. He knew she wasn't a criminal, at least not a *deliberate* criminal. It was simply her poor luck that she'd lost her wallet, cash and credit cards. Although she had no doubt she would get a stern lecture when her attorney heard about Jenny's spur-of-the-moment cross-country motorcycle trip.

"He's here." The waitress stuck her finger beneath

Jenny's nose and pointed out the window. "That's the sheriff. You're toast."

Jenny turned her head, dark brown eyes widening as she watched a shiny black police car pulling up in the parking lot. Her headache kicked into high gear. Her palms began to sweat. The door swung open and a pair of dusty cowboy boots hit the ground. Jenny had hoped for a kindly soul, someone who would say, "Golly, shucks," and have a good chuckle at all these misunderstandings.

Instead, she got the Gladiator of Bridal Veil Falls.

He stepped out into the fading sunlight, a full six-foot four inches of masculine intimidation wrapped up in a slim-fitting beige police uniform. His shoulders went on forever, his hips were narrow, his stomach tight and flat. She couldn't see much of his face; he wore a cowboy hat pulled low over his forehead. He also wore dark glasses. Jenny had never seen a jaw so square or a chin so intimidating. And those straight lips could have been chiseled from marble.

Jenny dropped her head into her arms on the table. "This is *not* my day."

The front door opened and closed. Jenny heard slow, measured steps growing louder and louder...until they stopped right in front of her. She couldn't bring herself to look up.

"Is this the one?"

His deep voice had a no-nonsense tone. There wasn't a trace of a friendly country accent. Jenny's optimism shriveled up like a grape in the sun. She wondered how old she would be before she got out of jail.

The waitress started spilling the whole story from the beginning. She concluded with a disdainful, "Funny thing, sheriff, how she didn't notice her wallet was gone until after she ate enough food for ten people."

"I resent that." Jenny looked up, glaring at the waitress. She couldn't bring herself to look at the sheriff quite yet. "I ate a well-balanced meal. You try hanging on to a runaway motorcycle for eight hours and see how hungry *you* get."

Came the unsympathetic voice of the sheriff: "So that Harley outside is yours?"

She took a deep breath, forcing herself to meet the sheriff's sunglasses squarely. "Maybe. At this point, I'm taking the Fifth on everything."

For a long, uncomfortable moment, he didn't say anything. At this close range, Jenny could see the manly dent in his manly chin. His slanted cheekbones were perfectly molded, his nose perfectly straight, his posture everything a Marine Corps recruiting poster could ask for. It must be true, she thought glumly, what everyone said about the healthful benefits of fresh country air.

The Gladiator pursed his lips and whistled softly. "What do you know? It's you."

Jenny frowned at him, wondering what he was trying to trick her into admitting. "No, it's not. I don't know what or who you're talking about, but I didn't do anything wrong. I'm just an innocent traveler who happened to lose her wallet. Believe me, I would have taken a detour if I'd known you people in Bride Falls on Her Head were so paranoid and unfriendly."

"Bridal Veil Falls," he corrected, a faint smile curling his lips. "You know, the minute I saw your red hair, I knew I was looking at trouble."

Jenny glared at him, then slid out from the booth, brushing tortilla crumbs off her jeans as she stood up. It was time she adopted a defensive attitude. She felt at a distinct disadvantage sitting. Still, at five foot two she didn't gain much height. If he put his arm out straight, it would go right over her curly head. "Let's talk about trouble. I was hungry, so I decided to stop and get something to eat. Before I know it, I'm being accused of all kinds of things I didn't do. At least, I didn't do them *intentionally*. I'm not some career criminal who travels from town to town on her motorcycle ripping off Mexican restaurants—" she threw the waitress a dark look "—despite what *she* seems to think. And I'll tell you something else."

"Oh, boy," the sheriff drawled. "She's not done yet."

"This town has trouble written all over it. Everyone here is *hostile*." She paused, then added grudgingly, "Well, that's not true. That sweet white-haired lady crocheting in the corner booth has been very friendly. She keeps smiling at me. I like her, but otherwise, I can't wait until I see the last of this place."

Obviously listening to their conversation, the white-haired lady waved her crocheting needles at the sheriff. "Hello there. You're looking very handsome in your new hat."

"Always the sweet-talker, Ella," the sheriff called out. Then he exchanged a speaking look with the waitress. "You didn't tell me my grandmother was in here today, Sunny. That kind of puts a new light on things, if you know what I mean."

"Sunny?" Jenny blurted out incredulously. "Her name is *Sunny?* She is the least friendly waitress I've met in my life. And that lovely lady is your grandmother? How weird is that?"

The sheriff took off his sunglasses, swinging them in slow circles from his finger. The blue-eyed gaze he lev-

eled at Jenny was heavy-lidded, thoughtful and pene-
trating. He had Baryshnikov eyes, luminous and startling
against the smooth, golden-brown tint of his skin. Far
more beautiful than she had expected. And much more
human.

"Her name is Sunny," he told her conversationally,
"and that lovely lady is indeed my grandmother. My
name is Sheriff Cook, but you can call me Tyler. You
see? We're actually a very friendly town, so you don't
have anything to worry about. Now do me a favor and
be quiet for a minute. If you're capable of it. Sunny,
how long has Ella been here?"

"Well...most of the afternoon," Sunny replied, looking uncertain. "I never thought about...well, Dr. Wetzel
told me she was doing better. Said she took up crocheting instead."

The sheriff ignored her, continuing his conversation
with Sunny. "Something tells me Ella has had a little
relapse. She looks too happy."

Jenny slapped her forehead with her hand. "What is
going on here? Am I going crazy? Or is everyone in this
town crazy *except* me? Why won't you let me go outside
and look for my wallet? What does that nice little lady
have to do with anything?"

The sheriff looked sideways at her. "Don't you *ever*
do anything you're told? I said to be quiet."

"I don't have to be quiet," Jenny said. "I'm in deep
trouble, anyway. What are you going to do, arrest me
for using up too much of your oxygen?"

He tipped his hat back on his head, revealing a tangled
fringe of honey-colored hair. "You have a really bad
attitude. I know your middle name is Trouble. You mind
telling me your first and last?"

"Jenny Kyle." She held his gaze, one golden brow arching defiantly. "Jenny *Maria* Kyle."

"You have the right to remain silent, Jenny Trouble Kyle." He folded his sunglasses and slipped them into his breast pocket. "Take advantage of that right, while I go and have a little talk with Ella."

Jenny immediately bristled. "That nice woman has done absolutely nothing to...*mummph.*"

The sheriff was pressing his fingers firmly against Jenny's lips. "The right to remain silent."

Jenny's eyes narrowed dangerously. From the tip of her head down to her toes, her entire body stiffened beneath his touch. Sunny giggled, finding the whole thing immensely entertaining.

"That's a good girl," Tyler said. He removed his fingers slowly, by inches, as if prepared to silence her again should she dare open her mouth. "Now, sit."

"I feel like standing." The words came out in a rush, before he could react.

It should have made him angry. She had *intended* to make him angry. Instead his lips crooked in a smile that might have been boyishly beguiling under different circumstances. "Trouble," he said softly, then walked away.

Jenny had no idea what he said to the poor, dear lady in the corner booth. They spoke too softly to overhear, no matter how hard she strained. She couldn't even see the woman's expression, since the sheriff's broad-shouldered back blocked her view. Jenny could only wait and wonder, her teeth working nervously at her lower lip.

When he returned to her, however, her chin was high and her unsteady fingers were hidden in the pockets of her jeans. She wouldn't give him the satisfaction of knowing he could shake her. She'd done nothing wrong, and she wasn't about to act as if she had.

But she might have been invisible for all the notice he paid her. He pulled Sunny aside and whispered something to her, nodding his head in Ella's direction. Sunny listened intently, then hurried to the telephone and made a call.

"I don't suppose you would like to explain to me what that was all about?" Jenny asked. "Wait a minute. I know! You're going to arrest that wonderful little woman for being too friendly. I'm sure that's a felony around here."

For a long moment Tyler didn't answer. He simply examined her leisurely, his head tipped to one side. "You know, you really have a problem with authority figures. I think a few years in the big house is going to do you a world of good."

She gave him her wide-eyed, vulnerable look. "A few years? The big house? What is this, a James Cagney movie?"

"And I don't see any sign of remorse for your crimes, either," he went on thoughtfully. "It doesn't look good for you, Trouble."

"Give me a break! I lost my stupid wallet, for Pete's sake!"

"Like I said, a real bad attitude." He sighed, shaking his head. "Judge Curry doesn't like anyone with attitude. He doesn't care much for anyone who rides motorcycles, either. Last Fourth of July a motorcycle gang came tearing through town, right in the middle of the Independence Day Parade. Flattened two flashing barricades and ran over Judge Curry's bulldog. He had him all dressed up for the occasion, too, with a red, white and blue collar and a little stovepipe hat. It was a real heartbreaker, I'll tell you.''

Now Jenny sat down, groaning as her head dropped against the back of the booth. "Wonderful. Just shoot me, would you? Shoot me and put me out of my misery."

"Of course, the judge does have a soft spot for women," he went on. "You could very well get out in a year or so on good behavior. You know any karate?"

She stared at him. "What?"

"Karate. You know, kickboxing and punching and things like that. Believe it or not, the women's correctional facility is a lot harder on the inmates than the men's. You'd be wise to brush up on your self-defense."

"Do you honestly think I'm buying this?"

He grinned, pushing his hat back another inch. "I don't really care if you believe it or not. Any family or friends you want me to call before I toss you in the slammer?"

The look she gave him was strangely blank. "What?"

"You're entitled to a phone call. Would you like to call your poor husband, God bless him?"

"You have such a delightful sense of humor," she muttered. "*If* I had a husband, which I don't, I'd be an idiot to use my one call on him instead of my lawyer."

"Suit yourself. Oh, I have something for you. With all the excitement of apprehending a dangerous criminal, I almost forgot." He pulled something out of his back pocket and tossed it on the table. "Look familiar?"

Jenny stared at her green wallet. Her jaw dropped like a stone. "Where did you get that?"

"Actually, Ella just gave it to me. She said to tell you that you have beautiful hair and she hopes she didn't cause you any trouble. She has a little problem with taking things that aren't hers. Ella's an angel, but she's a couple of beers short of a six-pack, if you know what I mean.''

Jenny felt like someone had put her backward on an upside-down merry-go-round. She stared at sweet little Ella, who was suddenly deeply absorbed in her crocheting. Then she turned her stormy gaze back to the devil disguised as a lawman. She slammed her fists on the table so hard, her wallet jumped two inches with pure terror. ''I don't *believe* this! You knew all along, didn't you? You conned me! You knew Ella had stolen my wallet, and you deliberately let me think—''

''I object,'' he said mildly. ''I haven't seen you think yet. Besides, Ella isn't really a thief. She just borrows things sometimes for excitement. She always gives everything back sooner or later. We thought we had her cured when she discovered crocheting. She loved it, never put it down long enough to pick anything else up, if you know what I mean. I guess we'll still have to watch her.''

His casual attitude infuriated Jenny. ''You deliberately tortured me, talking about dangerous women's prisons and dead bulldogs. You had no intention of arresting me. I should have *you* arrested!''

His vivid eyes sparkled. ''The dog didn't die. He just rolled over a few times and ruined his hat. Anyway, I'm the only law this town has, so I can't really arrest myself, can I? Think of the complications putting on the handcuffs.''

Through gritted teeth, Jenny told him, ''I'll help.''

''Oh, chill out. I was just teaching you a lesson. You needed an attitude adjustment.''

''An *attitude* adjustment?'' She was up and out of the booth with amazing speed, facing him down with the light of battle in her eyes. Or rather, facing him *up*. He was extraordinarily tall. "*I'm* the victim here! The only thing I'm guilty of is having a rotten day. I've been wrestling with that wretched motorcycle all day, and I'm completely exhausted. All I wanted when I stopped here was some food and a rest room. *Bam,* before I know it, I'm being treated like public enemy number one!"

He took a moment before he answered. "So you admit you have a few problems controlling that monster outside?"

Jenny was too angry to be cautious. "A few problems? The thing is possessed by the devil. I'm lucky to be alive."

His wide mouth quirked. "I believe you. I know a little something about motorcycles. That Harley is too much machine for you, Trouble."

"That's my problem, isn't it?" She grabbed her wallet, opened it up and threw a twenty dollar bill on the table. "There. My criminal career is ended."

"And a damn fine career it was," he said.

"And now, amazing as this experience has been, I feel the urge to hit the road. Excuse me, Sheriff. It's been a real treat."

He blocked her exit, one hip braced casually against the edge of the booth. In the depths of his eyes, there was an unmistakable mixture of amusement and sympathy. He held her gaze, rubbing his square jaw for a lazy moment. "Let's ponder those three words, shall we? *Hit the road.* Do you realize if you climb back on that motorcycle of yours, there is a very good chance you will do exactly that—*splat.*"

"Thank you for your concern," Jenny replied with saccharine sweetness, "but I don't want you worrying about lil' old me. I've had a lot of experience taking care of myself. Now, is there anything else you would like to accuse me of, or am I free to go? *Finally?*"

He pulled a stick of Juicy Fruit gum out of his pocket, slowly unwrapped it and put it in his mouth, as if he had all the time in the world. "You forgot to stand in line when they handed out common sense, didn't you? I'm afraid I can't in good conscience allow you and your motorcycle out after dark. It would be a much better idea if you waited until morning to hit the road. That way other motorists would have a sporting chance of survival."

Her eyes narrowed. It irritated her that he was standing so close, *confining* her, as if he had nothing to do for the rest of his life but make *her* life difficult. "It's not dark yet."

"Worse. It's dusk. More accidents happen at this time of night than any other. It's a documented fact."

"Well, document *this*. I have places to go, and you're holding me up."

His blue eyes opened wide, as if he'd just had the most ingenious thought. "You know, you seem like an adventuresome girl. Why don't you try something new? Be reasonable."

"I'm not the one being unreasonable," she snapped. "Are you going to let me out of here or not?"

"Lord, no."

"Sorry, Mr. Sheriff, sir. It's a free country and you don't really have a say in it."

He smiled, rocking back and forth on the heels of his well-worn boots. "Would you mind showing me your motorcycle license, ma'am? Just to make sure everything is in order?"

Silence. "My what?"

"License," he said softly.

"I have a driver's license—"

"*Motorcycle* license, ma'am."

Jenny closed her eyes and counted to ten. "I haven't gotten around to getting one yet. I've only owned the Harley for a couple of days. I'll take care of it when I go home."

"That won't do," he said almost apologetically. "I'm afraid I'm going to have to arrest you, ma'am."

"You're going to arrest me? For what? Forgetting to get a motorcycle license? Is that a felony around here?"

"It's very bad," Tyler said gravely. "*Very* bad."

Jenny tossed back her hair defiantly. "Ha! You're just trying to jerk my chain again. You're going to put me in jail for a little oversight? *That* I'd like to see."

But it happened so fast, she didn't really see anything. His hands moved quickly over hers, there was a flash of silver and an ominous click.

She was handcuffed.

"You have the right to remain silent," Tyler began. "You have the right to—"

"What?" Jenny was flabbergasted. A vein beat wildly in her throbbing temple, keeping perfect rhythm with her racing heart. "Are you nuts? You can't keep me here, and you know it! I could sue you for false arrest. I could have your badge. I could—"

"Now you made me lose my place," he grumbled. "I'll have to start all over. You have the right to—"

"If you think for one second that you're going to get away with this macho power trip, you've got another think coming. You picked the wrong—" Without warning, she felt herself being upended and tossed over his shoulder as if she weighed no more than a single little Mexi-fry. The red-and-white-checkered linoleum floor filled her bouncing vision.

"Women never take advantage of their right to remain silent," Tyler Cook said. He started to walk, one arm clasped tightly around the back of her knees. "I don't know why I even bother saying that part."

Two

In high school, it hadn't escaped Tyler Cook's attention that the local girls had a weakness for a lanky cowboy with summer-blue eyes and an all-American smile. They enjoyed the way he walked, real slow and lazy, like he had no place to go and nothing to do when he got there. His appeal only seemed to increase when he put on his cowboy hat, and the ultimate drawing card seemed to be the bruises and abrasions and black eyes he got whenever he competed in a weekend rodeo. Riding mean-tempered broncos wasn't exactly a safe or ordinary hobby, but he was young and relished the attention from the stands. Besides, he had a real talent for sticking like a burr to the back of a half-crazy bronco. Inevitably there were times when he ended up eating dust, but the sympathy he received from the buckle bunnies was ample compensation for a wide range of physical injuries. Tyler was young, curious and restless, and there were times when the pace of his small-town life got on his nerves. Like, *all* the time.

If truth be told, Tyler knew it wasn't so much Bridal Veil Falls that irritated him as it was his own father's attitude toward his only son. Gerald Cook believed that boys were to be molded with a heavy hand, and he had the heaviest hand in town. While Tyler's little sister, Rosie, was spoiled and indulged, Tyler himself was the target of constant criticism and harsh physical punishment for any perceived weakness. According to his father, this would make a man out of him. Which it may have done, but it also made Tyler determined to leave his hometown in the dust the first chance he got.

After graduation from high school, Tyler wasted no time packing up his Chevy truck and heading for college at Montana State University. He had an athletic scholarship, which, along with a part-time job and a government loan, enabled him to get an education far from his father's harsh disapproval. Unfortunately, his formal education came to an abrupt end ten months shy of graduation. His father had a stroke that prevented him from working the family farm. Tyler realized he had a responsibility to contribute to the family finances. Rather than go home and try to wring a pittance out of fifteen hundred acres of dry farm during a drought, he opted to join the rodeo circuit. Professional rodeo paid real well if you had a talent for it, and there wasn't a bronc in the world Tyler couldn't ride—saddleback or bareback. He had an empathy for wild things, possibly because he recognized some sort of long-suppressed wildness in himself. He sent home his winnings, though his father never openly acknowledged his son's hard-won success. Even Tyler's picture on the cover of *American Cowboy* magazine went unnoticed...or at least, unremarked.

The same day Tyler received the gold buckle proclaiming him the World Champion All-Around Cowboy, his father passed away from a second stroke. Though it was too late to come to an understanding with his father, there was no one else to look after his younger sister and grandmother, which necessitated his return to Bridal Veil Falls.

And so Tyler went home to uphold law and order, inciting a near riot among the unattached females of Bridal Veil Falls. For eight long years he dodged and ducked and sidestepped the avalanche of feminine attention, sweet potato pie and Toll House cookies continually coming his way while he waited for the right girl to come along. He knew exactly what he was looking for—someone he could chase until she caught him. How hard was that? She would be tall and willowy, with lustrous dark hair and an adorable dusting of freckles across her cute little nose. Oh, he'd know her the minute he saw her, that much was certain.

Which was why he was nearly knocked out of his Tony Lama cowboy boots when he walked into Enchilada Ernie's to arrest a criminal and found his soul mate.

There she was. *There she was.*

It was destiny at first sight. Tyler certainly hadn't expected her to come barreling into town on a Harley-Davidson, with wild copper hair and a "just try me" expression on her face, but there she was, anyway. She wasn't what he had expected all these years, but she was so much more. Barely five feet tall, with enormous doe-brown eyes shimmering over high cheekbones. Her tank top was tight beneath her studded leather vest. Her ears were triple-pierced. Her hands were perpetually clenched in frustrated little fists. Not the woman he had expected all these years, but damned if she wasn't the one he'd been waiting for all his life. Best of all, there was no predatory glint in her eyes, just a hectic, high-flying spirit that reminded him of his own. No, best of all she had a ring on every single finger except the all-important "she belongs to me" finger. Yippee!

Unfortunately, when sweet Ella had turned out to be the criminal, Tyler had been left with no way to keep his soul mate in town. Fortunately, a stroke of genius had prompted him to ask Jenny for her motorcycle license. It was a happy man indeed who walked out of Enchilada Ernie's with the woman of his dreams slung over his shoulder like a rather light bag of potatoes.

She didn't wear perfume. In fact, she smelled a little like motor oil and salsa, but he didn't mind that at all. Had she been able to see his expression while he walked to his patrol car, she would have seen the crooked, whimsical smile that had been pulverizing female hearts for years. But she couldn't see anything but the black asphalt parking lot, poor thing, and all her energy was going into squirming and shouting and pounding on his back with those frustrated fists.

"Settle down," he told her, trying to sound stern and commanding, rather than amused. "You're going to hurt your lovely petite self."

Jenny's chin bounced hard between his shoulder blades. "I'm not the—ugh!—the one who is going to get hurt. You're going to be so sorry you ever—"

"Listen, if you don't behave yourself, I might get the idea you're resisting arrest. You don't want to be charged with that as well, do you?" He set her down next to the passenger door, being careful to keep her arms pinned to her sides. "Face the facts, Trouble. You've just been put in protective custody, and there's not a damn thing you can do about it."

Jenny tossed her head so high her hair hit him in the face. "Protective custody? That's a joke. Just what are you supposed to be protecting me from? *Normal* people? I hate to tell you this, Sheriff, but you don't fall into that category."

His smile came ever so slowly, crinkling his eyes, denting one cheek and glossing him over with a heavy dose of country charm. He leaned forward, putting his mouth close to her ear. "I'm protecting you from yourself," he said softly. "I hate to break this to you, but *you're* not exactly normal, either."

Jenny swallowed painfully, rubbing hard on her neck where his breath had tickled her. She really didn't like anyone this close to her, invading her personal space and making her stomach feel as if a fist had grabbed hold of it. There was a disturbing warmth in his eyes, radiating through her skin and bones, heating her up way down inside. Instinctively she tried to back away, only to come up hard against an unyielding police car. "Thank you for your honesty. Now tell me how much it's going to cost me to get out of this motorcycle license thing. That's what you want, right? Some kind of bail money?"

That's not at all what I want, Tyler thought. But aloud he said, "I'm in such a good mood today, I'm willing to forgo the whole bail thing—on one condition."

Jenny's defensive little chin went up another notch. "Really? And what might that be?"

Tyler grinned. "I hope you don't think my interest in you is anything but official. I'm simply looking after your best interests. The road from here to Helena is murder if you're not familiar with it, one switchback after another. *Are* you familiar with it?"

Immediately she replied, "Yes."

"Liar. You wouldn't make it ten miles on that road before you plopped yourself and that nuclear scooter in the river."

"That's *my* problem."

Tilting his head thoughtfully, he slowly rocked up and down on the heels of his boots. "Well, now…that's where you're slightly confused. As a public official, I'm charged with the welfare of every man, woman, child and childlike woman in my jurisdiction. As long as you're in this town, you're my responsibility. In daylight the idea of you on that Harley is scary enough. But at night? No way are you leaving here tonight."

For a moment Jenny felt queasy. She had the unnerving sensation of being out of control, caught like a mouse in a trap. Her freedom was more important to her than food, air or water. "You can't force me to stay here overnight. You can't force me to stay anywhere."

"Not here in the parking lot," he agreed. "That would be cruel and unusual punishment. You have two options, Trouble. You can check into the Cotton Tree Motor Lodge or you can stay in our little jail. I wouldn't recommend the jail—the mattresses are like concrete. But the choice is yours. In the morning, after I give you a crash course on riding that Harley—no pun intended— you'll be free to leave. I'm a friendly guy, remember? As long as you cooperate, I won't even ticket you for not having a motorcycle license. See?" White teeth flashed. "I'm a very nice person."

She held his eyes for a silent, simmering moment. "You are a very *bad* person," she said, jabbing him in the chest with her finger. "This is blackmail, and you know it."

"Pretty much."

"And what's more, you're *enjoying* it."

"Right on that one." He grinned, deep grooves framing either side of his expressive mouth. "Can't put one over on you, can I? Which will it be, Trouble? Jail or the Cotton Tree?"

Jenny's hands slowly closed into fists at her side. She was trapped and she knew it, which made the situation even harder to swallow. Restraint suffocated her. Her cheeks were burning, but she never took her eyes away from his. "All right," she snapped. "I'll check into the Cotton Tree like a good little hostage. But come morning I'm out of here."

"Thank you *so* much," Tyler said, hand over his heart. "May I open the door for you?"

"What about my bike?"

"I'll have someone bring it over to the motel." He adopted a wide-eyed cherub's expression, which was enhanced by the tangled fringe of honey-bronzed hair beneath the brim of his hat. "In the morning, of course. I wouldn't want you sneaking out of town tonight when I wasn't looking. Motorcycle keys, please."

"You don't trust me?"

"Not at all. Keys?"

She retrieved the keys from her back pocket and slapped them into his waiting palm. "Do you mind if I get my duffel bag out of the storage compartment, or would you like to impound that, too?"

"Not at all." Dimple in gear, an amused Tyler tossed the keys into the air and caught them. "I'll be more than happy to get it for you. *After* you get in the car."

Jenny pushed his hand away as he reached past her to open the door. She opened it herself, teeth ground together hard enough to make her jaw ache. Giving him one last murderous look, she climbed in, slamming the door shut with astonishing force from such a petite woman.

She didn't see Tyler laughing. She couldn't; he had his face buried in his arms on top of the car.

Tyler was a realist. He knew he definitely had his work cut out for him.

He braked for a stop sign and glanced sideways at his unhappy captive, raising his eyebrows as he noted the sullen set of her lower lip. Apparently, she didn't think being arrested was romantic. She wasn't talking, she wasn't moving, he wasn't even sure she was breathing. Such a defensive little soul.

"Try to remember this is for your own good," he said cajolingly, trying to win a little smile. He'd never had trouble coaxing a smile from a woman. Until this woman.

Jenny sniffed disdainfully and slumped farther down in her seat. This was the first sign of life she'd shown since Tyler had started the car.

He tried again. "Bridal Veil Falls isn't such a terrible place to spend the night, you know. It's a nice little town."

At that, she laughed out loud. "I'm sure. Although it *should* have been named Bride Falls on Her Head, like some creepy town in a Hitchcock movie."

Tyler grinned, then took his right hand off the steering wheel, driving with his knee while he patted her shoulder. "Hey, don't knock it till you've tried it. If you give it a chance, you'll see that Bridal Veil Falls is a perfectly normal town. And who knows, you might like it so much you'll decide to stay."

"Yeah, right," Jenny replied. Unsettled by Tyler's casual touch, Jenny shifted away from him. "Now stop driving with your knee or I'll make a citizen's arrest."

He put both hands back on the wheel, slanting her a quizzical look. "I'm just a wild and crazy guy, I guess. You don't like to be touched, do you? Sorry. I was just trying to lighten the mood a little."

"I can handle my own moods," she muttered. "Since you're keeping me here against my will, I'm sure you'll understand if I don't want to become bosom buddies."

"Whatever you say." He turned into the parking lot of the Cotton Tree Motor Lodge, pulling up in front of a lighted soft drink machine. He kept the car idling, giving her a look of blue-eyed innocence. "Seeing as how you don't want to be friends, I won't inflict myself on you further by going in with you to register."

She gave him a look that said, "I didn't ask you to," then pushed open the door and climbed out. *Slam.* She opened the door to the back and pulled out her duffel bag. *Slam.* "For a little bit of a thing," Tyler remarked through the open window, "You swing a mean car door."

Ignoring him, she hoisted the strap of her duffel bag over her shoulder and headed for the office. A stinging-hot shower of resentment prickled at her from her head to her toes. She was staying in a place she didn't want to stay, for no reason other than it suited the overbearing sheriff of Bridal Veil Falls. The man took his job way, way, *way* too seriously.

"Hey, Trouble. One more thing."

She stopped, gritting her teeth as she slowly turned on her heel. "What?"

"Have a nice night. We aim to please here in Bride Falls on Her Head." His tawny head was hanging out the window, hatless and backlit with the dying glow of sunset. He looked like an adorable Boy Scout trying to do a good deed, but she wasn't fooled for a minute. "Let me know if you need anything."

She gave him the most insincere smile of her life, followed by the most insincere statement of her life: "It's been wonderful meeting you, Mr. Sheriff, sir."

She turned and walked into the office without another word. She had a rhythm to her walk when she was irritated, a sassy little strut that she gave full rein to. Had she looked over her shoulder, she would have gotten yet another surprise.

Tyler Cook was smiling as if Heaven itself had just shown itself to him.

It was a typical motel room. The mattress was extra-firm, except in the middle where it was extrasoft. The pillows seemed to be made of plywood, and the air smelled strongly of disinfectant. The only window provided an aluminum frame for the blinking sign of the bowling alley across the street. Ritz Classic Bowl. Lounge, Leagues and Open Play. Plenty of Fun for Everyone!

Jenny sat on the bed like a zombie and watched the motel room change colors along with the bowling alley sign: red, yellow, green, red again. There was simply nothing else to do. She'd already showered, made a trip outside in her ratty chenille robe to the soft-drink machine for a cola, and watched an ancient rerun of *Mr. Ed* on television. It was barely eight o'clock, and she was wide awake and couldn't sit still. Nights were especially hard for her. Everything seemed intensified when the world wound down, grew quiet and dark. Her restlessness. Her memories. That lonely, aching place called the future, always waiting for her. She took it one day at a time, but no matter how many days, months, years she crossed off, the future was always just as vast and just as empty. No matter how many tomorrows she put behind her, they never seemed to grow easier or less intimidating.

She needed to keep moving, and this motel room was not the place to do it. She liked to have her mind occupied with unfamiliar places, unfamiliar things, unfamiliar people. In fact, anything *unfamiliar* was oddly comforting. She never went to bed before midnight, anyway, and never slept more than three or four hours at a time. Regardless of how tired she was—and Lord knew tonight her muscles had no more strength than limp spaghetti—her soul perpetually resisted rest.

She stood up abruptly, dressing in a clean pair of jeans and a rather wrinkled white cotton peasant shirt pulled from her duffel bag. Five minutes later her still-damp hair was curling wildly in the breeze as she walked across the street to the bowling alley. The night air had a bite to it; she made a mental note to buy herself a warm coat before she left town in the morning. She was thinking about making a little detour into Canada for a couple of weeks. She'd never been there before, and she'd heard it was an incredibly beautiful country. Originally she'd had vague plans of wandering down south to the warmer climes of New Mexico and visiting an artist's colony she'd heard about, but she could always do that later. Plans were made to be broken, especially hers. Spending the night in Bride Falls on Her Head wasn't the end of the world. She had to sleep somewhere, so there was no point getting all worked up about it.

Or that's what she told herself. Still, it was hard to ignore the raw nerves prickling under her skin. Ordinarily Jenny found it easier to be indifferent than offended, but there was something about Tyler Cook that jarred her senses, making them unusually acute. He was somehow different from other people she had met. He stood out from the blurred, forgettable crowd. It might have been the power of his tantalizing features, his perception or his sense of the absurd, but somehow she knew he was a man to be reckoned with. Jenny had no interest in reckoning with any man. Besides, in some secret corner of her mind, she knew she would come up short in a confrontation with him. He'd proved it once already, and she wasn't going to give him the opportunity to do it again. No, she told herself. I won't think about the square-jawed man with the devil in his blue eyes. And that's the end of it.

She walked through the doors of the bowling alley into an explosion of light, laughter and deafening sound. The confusion and noise had a soothing effect on her, distracting her from her thoughts. She took a seat at the snack bar, a good vantage point from which to observe the good citizens of Bridal Veil Falls on a high-flying Friday night.

The lanes were all full, which didn't really surprise her. There couldn't be too much to do in a town this size. There were several teenage boys with their dates, a half dozen men in orange bowling shirts in league play and a few families bowling together. Everyone wore gosh-awful red-and-green bowling shoes. Jenny's gaze skimmed the laughing children and parents without focusing on individuals. Years of long experience had taught her that some things were better avoided.

Still, there was something about the young family bowling in the nearest lane to her that caught and held her attention. Two chubby little boys wearing matching

yellow sweatshirts and baggy, blue-striped shorts were
working as a team, huffing and puffing as they lugged a
heavy bowling ball halfway down the lane. There they
dropped it into the gutter with a resounding thud and
turned around to accept their parents' applause. The little
boys' blue eyes were shining like sequins.

Twins.

Try as she might, Jenny was unable to tear her gaze
away from those identical, adorable snub-nosed faces.
They couldn't be more than three or four years old. Their
hair was the same white-blond shade as the young
woman's seated at the scoring desk—eye-catching and
unusual.

Happy with their achievement, the little boys laughed
and shuffled their way back to their seats in bowling
shoes twice the size of their feet. Jenny saw that the laces
were undone, dragging behind them on the ground. Their
noses were both peeling with sunburn and each sported
a Band-Aid on one knee. That was the way it was with
twins. What happened to one always seemed to happen
to the other.

No. Not always.

The inward voice cut through Jenny's thoughts like
the blade of a knife. She shivered, biting down hard on
her lip. It was time to concentrate on something else,
anything else, the first thing that came to mind…

"Tyler, double-knot their shoelaces, will you? They
won't stay tied."

Hearing the instructions from the twins' mommy, di-
rected at the man sitting on the bench with his back to
her, Jenny's gaze stretched. The man had unmistakable
hair, glittering with rainbow shades of dark gold and
warm bronze. Unmistakable shoulders, filling out every
inch of a well-washed blue chambray shirt. He slid off

the bench, going down on one knee to tie shoelaces. Jenny saw a Greek god profile and a lean, law-abiding jaw. Unmistakably Sheriff Tyler Cook.

Good grief, he was the *daddy*. His resemblance to those little boys was amazing.

For a stunned moment Jenny couldn't draw air into her lungs. It had never occurred to her that the irritating enforcer of the law might be married, though she couldn't say exactly why. It might have been the way he teased her with those come-hither, beach-boy-blue eyes. Married men weren't supposed to flirt. They weren't supposed to smile the way he had smiled at her, showing off his boyish dimples and his cowboy country charm. He had deliberately misled her, that's what he had done.

If looks could kill, Sheriff Cook would have met a nasty end right there on the paisley commercial carpeting at the Ritz Classic Bowl. He must have felt the daggers shooting into his back from the snack bar. He suddenly turned his head and looked directly at Jenny. She didn't have time to turn away, she didn't have time to compose her expression. They locked gazes, and he had the bloody nerve to send her one of his quizzical, blistering smiles. He saw her shock but showed absolutely no sign of embarrassment.

A single thought came to Jenny—there had been way too many intrusive emotions for one day. It was time to /turn off. She felt as if she were shrinking, separating from all the lights and noise around her, withdrawing into a well-guarded, secret cocoon. She shot off the bar stool as if it were made of red-hot coals. Hands pushed deep in her pockets, she plowed through the bowling alley with her determined gaze focused on the exit doors. Someone had spilled popcorn on the carpet; she could hear it crunching beneath her feet. Her peripheral vision caught a flash of blue as Tyler moved in her direction. Swallowing hard, she quickened her stride to a jog, but he caught up with her a good twenty feet before she reached the doors. Naturally. She had him pegged as the type who always got his man, even when his man was a woman.

He parked his tall body directly in front of her, putting an end to her flight for freedom. His smile was wide, brash and unabashedly cheerful. "If it isn't my old friend, Trouble. This is about the last place I expected you to wander into."

Jenny thought about his little family not fifty feet away, happy and oblivious to his true nature. Her blood simmered. "I'm sure it is. It must have been quite a surprise for you."

"I like surprises," he said. "I always have. That's what makes ordinary life interesting—all the little, unexpected things. Besides, you just saved me a trip to the motel. I was about to go over and check on you. I had this nagging feeling you might try and skip town on me." He put his hand on her arm to stop her as she tried to duck around him. "What's your hurry? You seem awfully anxious to get through that door. I'm being nice. I haven't tried to arrest you once."

"The night is young," Jenny muttered, using two fingers to remove his hand from her arm. "Don't worry, Sheriff. I gave you my word that I'll stick around until tomorrow morning, like a good little prisoner."

"There's that touching thing again," Tyler commented, his mouth tucking thoughtfully to one side. "Is it just me you're allergic to, or all human contact?"

She looked into this stranger's eyes, rattled by the shadowed glimpse of compassion there. Insight, understanding, communication…she wasn't interested in any of the above. Warning bells erupted in her head, much louder than the commotion of the bowling alley. She opened her mouth to toss back a careless, flippant remark—she was very good at that—but to her surprise, her mind remained stubbornly blank. Her fingers plucked restlessly at the gauzy fabric of her shirt, knowing that her momentary confusion was obvious.

"Just an observation," Tyler said, a different tone in his voice. Ever so briefly he touched the back of his knuckles to her uplifted chin. His lips carried the faintest hint of a smile. "See? That didn't hurt so much, did it? Relax. When I'm not in uniform, I hardly ever bite."

His hand was right back at his side where it belonged, but Jenny could still feel the unsettling, gentle brush of his touch. If they turned out the lights in the bowling alley, the imprint would probably glow in the dark. Sheriff Cook seemed to have a radioactive force field. "I'll take your word for it."

"Really?" His eyes were smiling as he pursed his lips and whistled softly. "No argument or snappy comeback? I'm impressed."

"Wonderful. Since meeting you, I've wanted nothing more to impress you. Haven't you noticed?" Looking over his shoulder, she saw three blond heads turned curiously in their direction. Something changed in her voice. "You're holding up the game and you're delaying my departure. You better get back to your bowling ball."

He tipped his head sideways, a casual, nonthreatening, good-buddy sort of expression on his face. His taffy-colored hair drifted around his forehead in the smoky, fluorescent lights. "Why?"

"Why?" She gave him a peculiar look. "Because

that's what people do in places like this. They roll bowling balls. Good old-fashioned family fun.'' She put an unmistakable emphasis on *family*.

Amazingly, it didn't even faze him. ''No,'' he said patiently, ''I meant, why are you leaving? You just got here, and I'm pretty sure you don't have a date tonight or have plans to wash your hair or something. So why the hurry?''

Jenny couldn't understand his persistence. His wife and children were within shouting distance and still he smiled with that brilliant, imperturbable gaze fastened on her. ''Bowling alleys are kind of tame for a dangerous hell-raiser like myself. Besides, I don't think your wife and children should be exposed to the criminal element.'' *There,* she thought. Chew on that one for a while, Gladiator.

But instead of flushing, Tyler's expression went oddly blank. ''Who? My what? Oh Lord, don't wish *that* on me.'' He actually shivered. ''She's my sister. I'm here with my sister. I came along to protect everyone else from those miniature pit bulls of hers. They're proof positive that big things come in small packages.''

The tight little fist that had been clamped on Jenny's stomach relaxed a bit. Not his wife, not his children. There went her hopeful perception of him as a two-timing Lothario. He would have been much easier to deal with had his character been less than sterling. Now he was a thoughtful and considerate man who chaperoned his sister and her children to the bowling alley on a Friday night. This was horrible. ''Whatever,'' she muttered, her cheeks burning bright as she tried to ignore the lazy amusement sparkling in his eyes. ''It's certainly very sheriff-like of you, protecting all these helpless bowlers from those terrifying little boys. I'm surprised you're not wearing a gun.''

His gaze slowly traveled the length of her, while his damnable, sweetly teasing smile played with his lips. "Who says I'm not wearing my gun? It always pays to be—''

"It's past my bedtime," Jenny said abruptly, manufacturing a wide yawn. "Way past. We hell-raisers need a lot of sleep to keep us in tip-top condition. Happy bowling, Sheriff.''

But when she tried once more to leave, he did a quick sidestep and once more prevented her from escaping. The man was very quick on his feet. "I make you nervous, don't I?''

She stepped to the left; he stepped right along with her. Exasperated, Jenny folded her arms over her chest and threw up her determined little chin, looking him straight in the eyes. "Too much coffee makes me nervous," she said. "Motorcycles that are possessed by the devil make me nervous. Clogged toilets, split ends and ingrown toenails make me nervous. And that just about covers it. Now, if you'll excuse me, I'm putting an end to our wonderful conversation.''

But then came a new voice into the wonderful conversation: "Heavens to Betsy, if this doesn't do my little heart good.''

It was Tyler's sister, slipping up beside him and tucking her hand into the crook of his arm. She looked like an all-American Thoroughbred, with long legs encased in tight white jeans and a cloud of baby-fine ivory hair pulled away from the sides of her face with tortoiseshell combs. A black-and-white-checkered shirt was tucked into a narrow leather belt, emphasizing the smallest waist Jenny had ever seen. She wore absolutely no makeup at all, just the healthy glow of a sun-kissed complexion. She looked to be no more than eighteen years old, which would have made her—what?—around fifteen years old when she had her children? Saints alive. They seemed to start their families early here in Bridal Veil Falls.

She smiled at Jenny with mischievous blue eyes, the unusual, crystalline color identical to Tyler's. "Usually Ty has the *most* predictable effect on women. They make goo-goo eyes and pant and slip him phone numbers, but they never, *ever* brush him off like you just did. Obviously, you're a woman to be reckoned with. I'm going to like you."

"Rosie's very shy," Tyler said. "Can you tell? Go away, Rosie."

Rosie continued with her breathless chatter, happily oblivious to her brother's ominous scowl. "He told me he had arrested Julia Roberts this afternoon. Now I see what he meant. You resemble her, you really do."

"What do I have to do to get rid of you?" Tyler asked his sister. His smile was gone. Completely. "Can't you just be cooperative for once in your life?"

"I've been trying to get rid of *you* for six years," Rosie scoffed, dismissing him with an airy hand. "Still you insist on continuing with the overbearing brother routine. I've learned from the best, and I will not be ordered around." She turned back to Jenny with a lavish, approving smile. "Where were we? Oh, yes, Julia Roberts. You really are lovely, really. No wonder Tyler told me he was—"

"Go *bowl*, Rosie," Tyler snapped. A light of panic flashed in his blue, blue eyes.

"—going to keep you," Rosie said brightly.

Three

"**W**ill you look at her go?" Rosie commented innocently, observing Jenny's rapidly retreating back with limpid blue eyes. "She didn't even say goodbye. Dear me. Did I say something wrong, Ty?"

"'Will you look at her go?'" he imitated in a scathing falsetto. "'Did I say something wrong, Ty?' Damn it, Rosie, why can't you mind your own business? You have no idea what I'm up against here."

Rosie stood on her tiptoes and knuckled the top of his head with her fist. "You're a big, strapping boy, you can handle it. I have to get back to the terrible two. When you come back, grab the boys a couple of hamburgers from the snack bar."

"When I come back from where?" Tyler muttered, watching Jenny disappear through the front doors. He'd never seen a woman's rear end sway with such disdain. She had very fluent body language.

"Back from chasing her down," Rosie explained kindly. "I've never seen you doing the chasing before. This is so entertaining. Don't forget—two hamburgers. No onions, no mustard. No anything but catsup—you know how they like 'em. And grab me a drink, too. Well, go on. What are you waiting for?"

Tyler bared his teeth at his sister with a frustrated growl, then took off running toward the front doors. He actually felt sorry for Jenny. Rosie's not-so-subtle sense of humor took a little getting used to. He was half afraid Jenny would plant herself by the side of the highway and hitch a ride with the first trucker that came along.

Once outside, he stopped short. Jenny was nowhere to be seen. He couldn't figure out how she'd vanished so quickly. She hadn't had time to cross the street and make it back inside the Cotton Tree. So where was she?

He started jogging again, going back and forth along the rows of parked cars, even stopping once to flop down on his belly and look underneath the parked cars. This woman seemed to have a talent for pulling off disappearing acts.

And then he saw her.

The picture she made took him completely by surprise. She was sitting on the rear bumper of a Ford pickup at the far corner of the parking lot. Her shoulders were slumped, her hands dangled in her lap. Flickering light from the neon Ritz Classic sign colored her small figure with a ghostly rainbow of changing colors. As he stared at the unutterably weary angle of her neck and head, the realization came to him that she was fighting tears. He didn't know how he knew it, but he did.

She looked so small from this distance, like a porcelain doll overwhelmed by the bleak silhouettes of cars and trucks. And oddly exhausted. She was barely fifty feet from the highway; a tanker truck passed and her hair snarled around her head in a wild, wind-whipped cloud. It looked to Tyler as if she had intended to cross the road to the motel, only to make it this far before she ran out of energy.

His throat dry with a sudden anxiety, he started slowly walking toward her. She didn't hear him coming until he was practically at her side, then her head whipped up and she pushed herself off the bumper in a quick movement. Surprisingly, her eyes were dry, glittering and immediately defensive. No tracks of tears on her pale face, as he'd half expected. Tyler was momentarily off balance. He could have sworn she was crying.

"Don't tell me," Jenny said, her voice a bit huskier than usual. "Let me guess. I'm being arrested for leaving a bowling alley in a rude and abrupt manner. Don't shoot me, Sheriff. I'll go quietly."

Tyler smiled faintly. "That'll be the day."

"So I'm not breaking any laws?"

"Not if you don't count disturbing the peace of the sheriff."

"What a relief. For a minute, there, I thought you were going to revert to Stone-Cold-Steve-Austin mode and toss me over your shoulder again. Just so you know, traveling upside down makes me sick to my stomach."

Tyler was quiet for a long moment, his thoughtful gaze never leaving hers. "You never take a breather, do you?" he asked finally. "It's just one wisecrack after another. Why did you run out of the bowling alley like that? Rosie was just speaking her mind, she's that way with everybody. Her blunt honesty terrifies the men in this town, which explains why she spends Friday nights at the bowling alley with her brother."

Jenny leaned back against the Ford's tailgate for support, her arms folded over her chest. Closed, locked away and guarded. "Whatever. I promise I won't lose any sleep over it. Actually, your sister seemed like a nice person. Kind of hard to believe you two are related."

"You must have been a porcupine in a past life. Why do you bristle every time I try to make polite conversation? I'm a nice guy, Trouble. No threat at all."

"I'll take your word for it," she said, mocking him with her wide brown eyes and innocent voice. "I'm like that, completely gullible. Willing to believe anything. Just another empty-headed little woman for you to—"

"Give it a rest, kiddo," Tyler said quietly. "Nothing's going to happen to you. You're okay."

Any other sort of comment she could have handled easily. But the unexpected sympathetic comment unnerved her. She avoided his eyes, looping her thumbs in her jeans pockets and staring intently at the black asphalt. She counted four flattened wads of bubble gum in one square yard. "Of course I'm okay. I'm always okay."

Tyler sighed like a man heavily burdened with a puzzle he couldn't solve. "There you go again, getting all thorny and defensive on me. I'm not here to torture you, believe it or not."

"Then why are you here?"

"I just wanted to make sure you were all right." He paused, picking his words carefully. "You looked... lonely."

Jenny stared at him. Blunt honesty—she hadn't expected that. It must run in his family. The physical pain that constantly lived in her chest breathed with new fire, ragged heartbeats filling her throat.

Lonely?

Truth be told, she could hardly remember back to a

time when she had been anything *but* lonely. But she was acutely uncomfortable that he suspected it, that he had recognized it in her. When she had stalked out of the bowling alley, she had been propelled by righteous indignation and an all-too-familiar urge to leave everyone and everything behind. Once outside, however, and without any warning at all, the starless sky had suddenly become too dark and the night too cold and the motel across the street too far away. Too many hurdles to jump. She had sat down on the bumper of the nearest truck and closed her eyes, concentrating on suppressing the cold sickness inside of her. She just needed a little time, like a wounded animal who crawled in a cave to heal. But *he* had come along and pulled her back to reality before she was prepared to face it again.

"I want you to stay away from me," she said. "Please."

And then she pushed past him, her eyes on the neon vacancy sign of the Cotton Tree Motel. Sanctuary. That was where she needed to be right now, holed up in her room with the chain on the door and the curtains drawn. And tomorrow she would be gone from this place, on the road to somewhere new and blessedly unfamiliar.

Afterward she didn't remember seeing the oncoming car. One second she was furiously walking, thinking and planning, the next she was blinded by headlights, frozen in place like a startled deer trying to cross the road. There was a terrible roaring in her ears: it may have been herself screaming or Tyler shouting or the deafening screech of brakes.

Light and sound, then...nothing.

Tyler never let her out of his arms until they kicked him out of the emergency room at the county hospital.

And then he stood immediately outside the little white curtain that was pulled around Jenny's bed and shouted at the nurses who came and went, feeling as if he was dying by inches. His limited medical training told him Jenny wasn't seriously injured. Her vital signs were strong, and he'd detected no sign of broken bones. But she hadn't regained consciousness since the car grazed her, tossing her like a limp rag doll in a sickening somersault onto the soft shoulder of the road.

At that moment Tyler discovered what terror was. He'd faced wild broncos and crazed Brahma bulls, he'd been stomped on, tossed head-over-heels and dragged through the dirt...but never had he been afraid.

Until tonight.

He scarcely drew another breath until nearly an hour later, when Dr. Grady Hansen came out from the curtained cubicle and told him Jenny would be just fine.

"Fine?" Tyler barely recognized the strained sound of his own voice. Grady's professional opinion was less than reassuring. It was hard to look at someone you'd gotten drunk with in high school and think of him as a qualified doctor. "What do you mean, she's fine? What about all the blood on her face and hair? She wasn't even conscious. Did you see her knees, Grady? Her jeans were shredded. And her ankle was swollen. Did you see that?"

"I noticed it, yes."

"Then what do you mean *fine?* There was a knot on her head as big as a softball. You're not very observant, Grady. We need a second opinion—"

"Yell a little louder," Grady snapped, snagging a fistful of Tyler's shirt and dragging him out to the waiting room. "There are probably a few ladies in the maternity wing who didn't hear you."

"I need a doctor, not a damned comedian."

"*You* need a swift kick in the butt," Grady threw back, unimpressed. "That lady back in there needs a doctor. I'll be putting a few stitches in her elbow and right knee. I've also ordered X rays of her ankle. I'm worried about a fracture. And she *has* regained consciousness, so relax and go patrol the parking lot or something while I try and do my job, okay? If all goes well, you should be able to take her home in a couple of hours."

"Home?" Tyler said blankly.

Grady frowned. "She's a friend of yours, right? When you brought her in, I just assumed…"

Tyler closed his eyes, a wave of relief washing over him. The heavy crushing sensation in the vicinity of his heart finally began to ease. He dropped his body back against the wall, needing the support. "Yes. She's my friend. She just doesn't know it yet."

"Well, good. I can't release her unless I know she has someplace to recuperate. Go get yourself a cup of coffee, Ty. You don't look so hot." Grady turned away, then looked back over his shoulder and wiggled his eyebrows above his wire-rimmed glasses. "By the way—*love* the shoes, Sheriff."

Tyler looked down at his feet. He still wore the ancient red-and-green bowling shoes from the Ritz Classic. Technically speaking, he had just committed his first felony.

He decided against arresting himself. Instead he wandered down the hall to the windowless little room that served as a chapel and sat on a hard wooden bench for over an hour. He didn't exactly say a prayer of thanks for tonight's miracle, but he figured that somebody somewhere understood exactly what he was feeling.

Jenny didn't remember much.

She knew she'd been at the hospital for a time. She recalled talking to a youngish doctor with a droll smile and a reassuring voice. She definitely remembered somebody saying, "This is going to sting a little bit," as they scrubbed the gravel out of her knees. And she remembered that it had stung more than a little.

At some point a nurse wearing green scrubs had given her a shot in the hip, and Jenny had drifted away in a lovely chemical trance, completely free of pain. End of memory.

A few minutes, a few hours, a few days later, she opened her eyes again. She saw nothing but a bright white light, obscenely bright. She found a blanket beneath her fingers and pulled it up over her head, trying to escape the light. When she emerged again, she did it by painful inches, coming out into the world like a new chick hatching from an egg. She realized several things all at once. She was wearing a completely indecent and undignified hospital gown and nothing else. It was daylight. Most startling, however, was the life-size clown with a shock of orange hair and purple-striped pants floating in the air above the bed.

As her foggy brain cleared a bit, Jenny realized she was looking at a stuffed toy dangling from a giant hook on the ceiling. She looked to her left and saw orange wicker shelves crowded with clowns of every size and every description. She looked to the right and saw a glossy six-by-four poster of a…clown. The bold caption at the bottom read, No Bozos Allowed.

So this was what happened when you died and had too many black marks next to your name. Saint Peter locked the pearly gates against you and sent you to clown hell.

Her vision was growing blurred when the door swung open and Tyler Cook joined her in circus purgatory. He was wearing a blue terry bathrobe and had wet, wild hair hanging down into his eyes. The robe dangled open in a wide vee over his chest and stomach, then was crossed and belted dangerously low on his narrow hips.

He stared at her intently, obviously startled by her tears. "You're crying," he said, dumbstruck. In all the painful procedures at the hospital, she had never shed a tear, nor uttered a single *ouch*. She'd been a rock.

"Am I?" Blinking in confusion, Jenny touched her cheek. Yes, her fingers came away wet. "I didn't realize. Strange." She frowned. "What happened to me? I'm feeling…really confused."

"You're probably still in shock. You don't get hit by a Pontiac every day." Though he tried to sound bright and bracing, Tyler was still suffering the fallout of witnessing her accident. He'd seen one or two bad accidents in his career as the sheriff, but he couldn't remember a time when he had felt more helpless. He'd seen the car coming at Jenny and had known instantly that he couldn't get to her in time. He simply had to watch it happen. The horror and sickening fear was still with him, slipping beneath his skin and keeping him constantly chilled. "You gave me a pretty good scare." A vast understatement.

"My brain is all foggy." Jenny tried to rub her eyes, then discovered the pads of her fingers were raw and sore, as if they'd been rubbed across a cheese grater. "What did you say? A *Pontiac* hit me? Well, of all the dumb—*ouch*, my poor hands…"

Tyler couldn't quite gauge the degree of her consciousness. She'd come to a couple of times on the way home from the hospital, but never seemed to be completely coherent. She had the same glazed look in her eyes now as she'd had in the emergency room. White face, overbright dark sequins for eyes.

"We'll backtrack a little," he said gently. "I just brought you home from the hospital a few hours ago. You don't remember being in the hospital?"

"I remember...yes, I remember the hospital. And I remember being in a bowling alley. But after that..." She paused, frowning. "No, it's sort of fuzzy after that. I don't remember a car hitting me, Pontiac, Chevy or Ford. Although I feel like I took on all three. My whole body hurts." Then, in a different voice, "Do I *bowl?*"

"Well, you didn't last night." Tyler dredged up a wan smile, trying to look reassuring. Still, something about her glazed expression kicked his heart into double-time. "You were just visiting. You're not in a league or anything, so relax. It's all right, everything will fall into place with a little time."

"What about..." She paused, trying to make some sense out of the quagmire of her scattered memories. "I remember meeting you at the Mexican restaurant. You wore some kind of a uniform, didn't you? You're a forest ranger or something. Your name is Tyler..."

"Actually, I arrested you in the Mexican restaurant. And I'm the *sheriff,* not a forest ranger. Forest rangers have to wear ridiculous green shorts, which I would never even consider. Yes, my name is Tyler Cook. See? Things are coming back to you. For a minute there, I thought you were suffering from some kind of post-traumatic—"

"How did I get there?"

Tyler shook the wet hair out of his eyes to study her better. "What? How did you get where?"

Jenny's huge eyes looked like painful bruises in her pale face. "That place, that Mexican restaurant. Did I come with someone? I remember a little lady with white hair…"

"Ella," Tyler said in a hollow voice. "No, you didn't come with Ella. Come on, *concentrate*."

"I don't have anything to concentrate *on*." Jenny had just delved deep into her mind, pre-Enchilada Ernie's, and come up completely empty. Completely, totally, shockingly empty. "I'm not kidding. I'm going into panic mode here. I'm trying, but…" There was a short pause, then she said accusingly, "Wait a minute. You *threw* me over your shoulder! You carried me out of that restaurant like a sandbag. What could you have been thinking?"

"I was thinking that I'd just arrested you!" Then, defending himself, "You weren't going willingly. You weren't at all cooperative."

"Why did you arrest me in the first place?"

She was becoming agitated, which wasn't good for her. Tyler sat down gingerly on the edge of the bed, making sure not to jostle her. She was confused enough as it was. "I don't know where to start. Let's see… First you ate dinner at Ernie's and couldn't pay for it. Then I found out you didn't have a motorcycle license."

"I'm a criminal?" She absorbed this for a moment, wide-eyed and apprehensive. "I don't feel like a criminal. I'm not a Hell's Angel or anything, am I?"

"That depends on your definition," Tyler said wryly. "Personally, I think *Hell's Angel* describes you perfectly. But no, you were traveling alone when I first saw you. And you're definitely a novice biker. You don't know the first thing about motorcycles, with the possible exception of how to kill yourself on one."

"But I ate when I couldn't pay for it?"

"Not exactly. You ate and then couldn't find your wallet. Remember that nice lady, Ella? She has a little problem with intermittent kleptomania. Fortunately, sooner or later she gives everything back to its owner. Does any of this ring a bell?"

"Yes! Yes, I *remember*," she breathed softly. "And that wicked waitress of the west was absolutely abominable to me."

"I think you might have seen *The Wizard of Oz* too many times." Tyler was feeling a little better now. Obviously, she was just out of focus because of her concussion. Fortunately it all seemed to be coming back to her. "See? No need for panic at all. You're fine. Although I do need to know who I should contact about your accident. I was going to run a check on your motorcycle license info, but...I was busy at the hospital threatening your doctor all night. Who would you like me to call?"

On a wispy strand of breath, "Who?"

"Your family. You told me you weren't married, but there must be someone worrying about you somewhere."

"My family? They're...I'm not...I don't remember who..."

"Jenny *Kyle*," Tyler prodded gently. "Your last name is Kyle."

"I know that," she said. And she did.

But that was *all* she knew.

It hit her all at once. Everyone had a family, right? Of course she had a family. Somewhere. And they probably had names and she probably had a wealth of lovely family memories stored away in the attic of her temporarily out-of-order mind. But as hard as she tried, she couldn't come up with anything. It was as if she had been born in the corner booth at Enchilada Ernie's.

"Oh-oh." With no warning, the entire room suddenly took off in a swirling waltz. Jenny groaned, her sickly color matching the shade of her white pillow case. "I just found something to concentrate on. I'm going to be sick."

Tyler grabbed for the empty wastebasket in the corner and handed it to her. "Here, use this." He sprinted into the bathroom, wet a washcloth with cold water and brought it back to Jenny. "Use this, too. On your forehead."

Jenny did as she was told, concentrating fiercely on maintaining control of her stomach. "I'm all right. I'm fine. But you better do something about your robe pretty quick. It's going south fast."

Tyler looked down and discovered he was about two inches away from becoming a centerfold. He muttered a word beneath his breath that had four letters, fastening his belt with a double knot. He didn't have time to deal with things like indecent exposure. He was flat-out panicked, close to being sick himself. She hadn't been kidding. She couldn't tell him who her family was. Still, she'd just barely opened her eyes, and she was seriously medicated with pain pills. She might just need a little encouragement. "Jenny? You know your name, so you must remember your family, and your…your life. Just calm down. Breathe, and be very, very calm."

"I remember something," she muttered, cradling the wastebasket in her arms like a life preserver. "I do."

"Excellent."

"I remember that I don't like to be told to calm

down.'' She opened her eyes, a flicker of her old spirit clearly evident. ''I'm certain of it.''

I need to pop a couple of her pain pills, Tyler thought. I'm coming unglued here. ''Maybe we're going about this in the wrong way. You do remember being at Ernie's. Do you remember anything from before you were at Ernie's?''

''No.''

An edge of desperation sharpened his voice. ''Sure you do. Just try.''

''I *am* trying. No, I don't remember anything before going to the restaurant. You're talking too loud. I have a terrible headache. It punishes me every time I try to think. Is this your house?''

Tyler was taken off guard by the change of subject. ''What? Yes, it's my house. But we're not talking about houses here, we're trying to ascertain—''

''Why do you decorate it with clowns? It's bizarre. You're a grown man.''

He bristled. ''And I have a very grown-up bedroom down the hall done in beige and black. This room is reserved for my nephews when they come over. You remember them?''

''I think so,'' she said, her voice suddenly weary. ''Yes…the twins, and your sister, Rosie. I remember your family. I just don't remember mine.''

Tyler dug up every ounce of his willpower to disguise the fear that was flooding him. He didn't want to scare her. He pasted a fake smile on his face and started backing up toward the door. ''We're pushing things. The doctor in the emergency room said you might be confused for a couple of days. It's normal for a concussion.''

''*This* confused?''

"Well...yes, of course. You're doing well, every bit as confused as the doctor expected. You're right on track. I have to go now, but I'll check on you in a little bit. I need to get ahold of your doctor and tell him something."

Jenny couldn't decide whether to cry or throw something or simply go back to sleep. "What? Tell him what?"

"Later," Tyler said, stepping into the hall and closing the door behind him. Then he slumped against the wall, his head making a hollow *thwack*. Beneath his breath he muttered, "I need to tell him that he's under arrest for impersonating a qualified doctor."

Four

Grady and Tyler were hiding in the bathroom across the hall from Jenny's room. Tyler insisted on taking precautions; he didn't want her to hear them discussing her amnesia.

"You've got to be kidding me, man," Grady said in an indignant whisper. "You're trying to tell me it's my fault she has a fuzzy memory after getting hit by a car? I fail to see how that can be remotely attributed to my medical skills."

"You examined her a few minutes ago," Tyler whispered back fiercely. "Did she seem all right to you? Could she answer any questions about her past? Are you *sure* you have a medical degree?"

Grady whipped off his glasses, glaring at his best friend. "I've had enough of this. I was in an important consultation when you called me. I did you a favor by coming over here and looking at her. And I'm telling you the woman has a concussion. Give her forty-eight hours and then panic if she's still a little vague about her past.''

''A little vague? She's blank!''

Grady sighed heavily, sitting down on the closed toilet lid. ''Look, I admit this isn't completely normal with head injuries like this. She remembers you, a perfect stranger, she remembers Ella, but she doesn't remember her own past. There is such a thing as selective retrograde amnesia, but honestly, you may be getting worked up over nothing. Give her a couple of days to recover from her accident, all right? After forty-eight hours, she'll probably be right as rain.''

''Right as rain?'' Tyler muttered. ''What the heck is *that* supposed to mean? Did you learn that in med school?''

Grady stood up, placing both hands over his ears in a most unprofessional fashion. ''I'm not listening to you anymore. Lose the shining armor for a while, Tyler. I know you're one of the good guys, I know you feel compelled to look after the whole world, but curb yourself for a couple of days. Any serious problems, get her over to the emergency room. Goodbye.''

Grady shut the bathroom door behind him, leaving the toilet seat free. Tyler sat down, arms resting on his thighs and hands dangling between his knees. He was so damn *frustrated*, he could hardly think. First of all, he was not a good guy by choice, and he was sick and tired of being tagged with the title. He was a sheriff because the job paid more than anything else in the farming community of Bridal Veil Falls. Which probably made him an opportunist, but try telling anyone else that. He looked after people because it was his responsibility, not his chosen calling. He lived in the back of beyond because he had

no choice. And he had Jenny Kyle in his spare bedroom
because that was exactly where he wanted her. Did that
sound like a knight in shining armor? Hell, no.

"I am *not* a good guy," he said to the floor.

And for once, no one argued with him.

Tyler left Rosie sitting with Jenny, then went to work
and had a day. Not a good day or a bad day, just an
ordinary, nothing-ever-changes-in-this-town day. There
had been nothing more challenging to investigate than a
telephone tip that thirteen-year-old Willard Wallin was
after George Sanders's homing pigeons with his BB gun
again. So, after Tyler had impounded Willard's gun for
twenty-four hours, he had plenty of time to think about
Jenny.

Tyler wondered if she had remembered anything yet.
He called Rosie, who told him Jenny was still sleeping.
He had a tuna melt at the café for lunch, then went back
to his office and called Rosie again. Once more she told
him Jenny was still sleeping, and she wasn't about to
wake the poor woman up and ask her if she had remembered anything. Tyler did some paperwork for an hour
and called Rosie one more time. His sister had a temper,
and she used it to the best of her ability. *Yes,* Jenny was
still asleep. Yes, she had checked to see if she was all
right. And for his information, Tyler's phone call had
woken the twins from their naps, which was a personal
tragedy for her. The only time she ever had to herself
was nap time, and he had robbed her of it. She hoped
he was happy. *Click.*

Tyler distracted himself that afternoon by playing
hangman with the mayor's son, who was in jail for stealing tires off the high school principal's car over the
weekend. The mayor thought a couple of days in the

slammer might teach the kid a lesson. Tyler didn't mind; he was actually grateful for the company. At precisely five seconds before 5:00 p.m. he left the office to his deputy and climbed back in his squad car for the six-minute drive home. He made a stop at the Cotton Tree for Jenny's duffel bag, taking a moment to search the contents for some clue as to her background. It was the damnedest thing. She carried only a few clothes, a wand of mascara, a hairbrush, a blow dryer and one single business card: Eliot Dearbourne, Attorney at Law. No less than three telephone numbers were listed at the bottom, all with a California area code. To say that he was surprised was an understatement. Never in his life had Tyler seen a woman who traveled so light. It was truly as if she had been born at Enchilada Ernie's. And speaking of Ernie's, when he drove past the restaurant, he saw Jenny's Harley and realized he'd forgotten all about it.

He couldn't say why he pulled into the parking lot. And he sure as hell didn't know why he got out of his car and walked around the Harley in a slow, lazy circle. He had to admit, it was an incredible machine. He'd had a dirt bike in high school, but nothing like this. This was a bike worthy of James Dean. Hell on wheels.

He really didn't remember making a conscious decision to trade his freshly waxed squad car for the mean machine covered with road dust. One minute he was staring at the Harley, the next he was tossing his cowboy hat in the back seat of his car, digging out Jenny's keys from the glove box and tugging off his beige shirt to reveal a plain white T-shirt beneath. For a minute he was caught by the image of his own reflection in the car window. Wild hair, muscle-skimming cotton tee, black sunglasses and a motorcycle standing by. He didn't look like himself, but he *felt* like himself. This was the Tyler

Cook he used to know a long time ago. His restless wild heart was still beating beneath the breast of the responsible adult. Feeling a little self-conscious, he looked over his shoulder. No one was watching the sheriff of Bridal Veil Falls.

A slow, "just watch me now" smile spread across his face. His eyes crinkled, his dimple made an appearance, and his white teeth gleamed wickedly against his bronze skin. He loaded Jenny's duffel into the storage compartment, alongside a little surprise he had picked up at the Happy Valley Drugstore at lunchtime. Presents were good. Women liked presents.

He gave the Harley one more look of 100 percent masculine appreciation, top to bottom, front to back. His smile felt as if it was tattooed on his face. Boy, oh, boy.

He felt like a cowboy again. He was just taking on a different kind of horse.

Jenny had slept most of the day. She vaguely remembered Rosie coming in and helping her exchange the hospital gown for one of Rosie's own frilly pink nightgowns. Then it was back to dreamland, until an unearthly roaring sound interrupted the peaceful silence of the sunlit bedroom. *Vrooom.*

She sat up slowly, knuckling her sleepy eyes. *Vrooom, vrooom.*

She cautiously swung her legs over the bed, waiting to see if her equilibrium was still AWOL. The throbbing in her bandaged ankle reminded her she was temporarily one-legged, but at least the Tilt-A-Whirl bedroom had stilled. She realized that she was absolutely drenched in pink bows and ruffles, a style of dress she instinctively knew she had never favored. Still, she was grateful for Rosie's generosity. That barely there hospital gown had provided very little coverage of areas most important to cover. Not to mention an uncomfortable draft.

Vrooom, vrooom, vrooom. Even louder this time.

Her curiosity got the best of her. She stood up and took giant hops to the window, grimacing with every jarring landing. Ankle, hands, head, ribs, everything made of bone or sinew protested fiercely—but she was too far along to turn back now. The window was open a few inches to let in a soft breeze, as well as the noises from outside. Oscillating lawn sprinklers. Kids laughing and playing dodgeball in the street. A dog barking. A summer evening scented with lilacs and fresh-cut grass swirled through the billowing curtains, casting a warm, murmuring spell. *Va-va-va-vroom.*

Startled, Jenny did a one-legged jump. Her gaze dropped to the driveway directly beneath her window. At first she saw only a strange man sitting astride a motorcycle. He was something else to look at, actually, a stunner with thick, wind-whipped hair, wraparound sunglasses and a white T-shirt that set off an enviable tan. His legs straddled the bike with easy grace, both feet on the ground balancing the powerful machine. He seemed utterly absorbed with revving the Harley's engine, then cocking his head and listening intently to the rhythmic purr.

"Will you quit with the macho motorcycle demonstration?" A door slammed, then Rosie sprinted down the front walk. "Jenny's still asleep, Ty. Or at least she *was.*"

Tyler? Jenny thought. That tawny-haired rebel on a bike was Sheriff Gladiator?

"No way," she whispered, eyes round as saucers.

The motorcycle's thunderous engine died a quick death. "Sorry." Tyler grinned at his sister, not at all sorry. "Boys will be boys. This engine is amazing. It took me only three minutes to get here from Enchilada Ernie's. Three minutes, Rosie. Damn, that felt good."

"You broke the speed limit?" Rosie asked incredulously. "You?"

"I *shattered* the speed limit," Tyler told his sister smugly. "There wasn't a soul on the road, so it wasn't like I was a threat to anyone. Besides, who's going to arrest me? Me? Anyway, this is Jenny's bike and I couldn't leave it sitting in town forever." He swung his leg off the Harley and stood up, towering over Rosie's five-foot frame. "I need to wake her up and tell her that her Harley is safe. I'm sure she'll be greatly relieved. Don't you think that's a good reason to wake her up?"

"She doesn't even remember she *has* a Harley," Rosie pointed out.

"Details, details," Tyler said. Whistling, he opened the storage bin on the back of the Harley and pulled out a duffel bag and a small sack.

"You're incorrigible, and I'm going to strangle you one day," Rosie told him sweetly. "Not today, because I have the boys with me and don't want to traumatize them. But someday."

"Whatever makes you happy, sis," Tyler said with an angelic smile. "I'm feeling very cooperative tonight. It's amazing what hitting 130 miles per hour on a Harley can do to one's perspective."

"You didn't!"

"I did. I went very fast on a very loud machine. What a rush. Breaking the law can be really exhilarating, if no one's around to get hurt. I haven't had that much fun since I stopped getting tossed off horses for a living."

"Have you been drinking?" Rosie demanded, slapping her hands on her nonexistent hips.

"Hell, no. Who would need to drink when you have a Harley between your legs? It's kind of the same principle of riding a bronco or a Brahma bull—highly diverting. Not to mention the fact I have a drop-dead gorgeous redhead in my clown bedroom. Life hasn't been this interesting in a long time."

Jenny leaned back against the wall, feeling guilty for eavesdropping, but not quite guilty enough to walk away from the open window. He thought she was drop-dead gorgeous?

Then, with a belated mental shock—he rode Brahma bulls?

"Tyler..." Rosie's voice sounded a bit troubled, unusual for someone who normally took life with a grain of salt. "I probably should mind my own business, but Jenny's life is an empty canvas right now. Getting personal might be a little...premature."

"And not at all prudent," he replied in a breezy tone. "The problem is, I'm just not feeling prudent lately. Go figure. One day I walk into Enchilada Ernie's and everything just..."

Their conversation faded away as Tyler and Rosie disappeared inside the house. For a long moment Jenny remained immobile. Since her life started only a couple of days earlier at a Mexican restaurant, she couldn't really say if she had much experience with affairs of the heart. She tried to understand and label the unfamiliar emotions rippling through her, but she had nothing to compare them to. She was surprised. She had inspired a man like Tyler to *not* be prudent? The thought gave her an odd little thrill of satisfaction. Strangely, she didn't feel too concerned about the fact that she was only two days old. That would solve itself. For whatever reason, her mind didn't want to settle and brood on her current predicament. She only had today, but today was enough to deal with right now. Very possibly she was the most contented amnesiac on record. Still, she simply couldn't pretend a fear or frustration she didn't feel.

She heard a soft knock on the door and realized Tyler had made it up the stairs in record time. She bolted for the bed, but realized too late that bolting had been a very bad idea. To save herself from falling flat on her face, she had to put weight on her injured ankle. She squealed with pain just as she reached the edge of the bed.

"What?" Tyler barged into the room, blue eyes blazing with anxiety. "Are you all right? What's wrong?"

Jenny collapsed on the edge of the bed, her eyes screwed shut, her face contorted in pain and her fists drumming the mattress. After a moment her pain subsided to a dull, bearable throb, and she opened her eyes to see that Tyler carried a duffel bag in one hand and what looked like a stuffed animal in the other. "Hello. Don't worry, I'm fine. I forgot I wasn't supposed to put any weight on my ankle."

Tyler raked his hand through his hair, blowing out an exasperated breath. "You know what Grady said this morning. Baby it for a couple of days. No testing."

"I realize I'm coming up a little short right now on my background, but somehow I don't think I've been used to staying in one place very long. Sitting still doesn't seem to be my strong suit."

"You've got that right," Tyler said with feeling. He was doing his best not to let his gaze dwell too long on the colorful garden of bruises on her face. She looked so small and fragile, as if she would shatter if anyone touched her with the slightest force. She also looked, he realized belatedly, very, very pink. "That's quite the nightgown you have on there. Extremely feminine."

"I look like a pink wedding cake with too much frosting. Still, I'm grateful to your sister for lending it to me. She's been incredibly sweet. Although," she added confidingly, "I don't think I wear ruffles and lace as a rule. They don't feel normal to me. It will be very interesting to go home to my wardrobe and find out. Wherever home may be."

"I take it you didn't wake up with all the missing pieces in place?"

Jenny felt oddly unnerved at his gentle smile, particularly since discovering he thought she was drop-dead gorgeous. She took refuge in careless banter. "Actually, I did. My name is Ophelia Detweiler, and I was serving five to ten for armed robbery when I stole a Harley from one of the guards and escaped."

Tyler dipped his chin and gave her a "very funny" look. "Well, at least you're keeping a sense of humor. I guess that's something." He placed the duffel bag on the bed beside her. "I thought you might need a few things. You do travel light, don't you?"

Jenny shrugged. "I guess so. Jenny Kyle seems to be kind of a weird duck, doesn't she?"

"You're taking it well, Ophelia, this little memory lapse you have."

"I don't see the point of getting too worried, since your doctor friend told me it was normal to be fuzzy for a couple of days after an accident. You're the one I feel sorry for. You've ended up with a pink, black and blue amnesiac, when all you really wanted was a prisoner. I really do feel much better now. I could probably go back to the Cotton Tree and—"

"No," Tyler said abruptly. "You're my responsibility. Besides, I took it upon myself to drive your Harley home—"

"I noticed."

"—*and* decided it was way too powerful a machine to let you loose on it, particularly when you're injured. So we'll just be patient until you're healed." And since he didn't want to argue with her, he decided to distract her. Holding the stuffed animal by its little tail, he dangled it in front of her nose. "I brought you a present. I saw this in town today and it reminded me of you."

"A present?" Jenny repeated softly. She felt incredibly strange, as if this was the first time in her entire life anyone had given her an unexpected gift. Somehow she knew that it wasn't something that had happened often to her lately. She took it from him, her fingers feeling clumsy. "You didn't need to do that."

He grinned, rocking back and forth on the soles of his feet as if he were very pleased with himself. "You like?"

She gave the fluffy little beast a long look. "This was very nice of you. It's a...well, it's a sheep, isn't it? I'm not sure what to say. I remind you of a sheep?"

"Look closer."

After a moment Jenny discovered all was not as it appeared. The sheep's nose and ears turned out to be a mask, and the wooly white sheep suit was completely removable. Underneath the ordinary sheep was a grinning wolf. "It's like a Halloween costume for wolves!" she laughed, charmed by the surprise. "Now I'm really curious. I remind you of a wolf masquerading as a sheep?"

Tyler sat down beside her on the bed, being careful not to jar her injured ankle. "Give me a little credit. This little sheep-wolf reminded me that people sometimes wear disguises for the rest of the world. Then, when they feel safe, they gradually reveal who they really are.'' He grinned widely, nudging her elbow lightly with his. ''You didn't know I was such a deep thinker, did you?''

Tyler Cook revving a Harley was a masculine force to be reckoned with. Tyler Cook letting loose the full power of his come-hither smile at a distance of barely eighteen inches was enough to send a poor sheep-wolf into cardiac arrest. The air between them seemed to instantly heat up by a good ten degrees. *Oh, Grandma, what pretty teeth you have...*

The magic of his smile unnerved her. Her physical reaction to that smile doubly unnerved her. Jenny stared at him unblinkingly until her eyes began to water. Then she quickly looked down at the masquerading wolf in her lap. ''Thank you for the present,'' she said stiffly. ''And for my clothes. It will be good to shower and dress. Do you think if I'm careful to keep my ankle—''

''Why do you do that?'' Tyler asked abruptly. ''For a moment we're talking like friends, then something happens and you're closed up and gone, just like that.''

''I don't know why,'' Jenny said lightly, still avoiding his gaze. ''I guess it's just something I do. That's the problem with being born yesterday. It's hard to figure out why you do the things you do when you don't have any history.''

''I'm serious here.'' Tyler lifted his hand to her cheek, turning her head gently toward him. The humor was gone from his blue-eyed gaze, the charming smile just a memory. An intense emotion darkened his eyes. ''Can't you just relax now and then? I don't bite. I'm not an ax murderer. I've taken a shine to you, Jenny Kyle. And I wouldn't hurt you for the world.''

Jenny was silent, her mouth dry, her pulse hammering in her temples. A little voice told her to immediately back off from Tyler's touch. A little bigger voice told her it felt so nice, and she should stay. She saw, fascinated despite herself, that Tyler's face was coming closer. His expression was intense, dark, acutely absorbed. His fingers spread on her cheek, warm and dry and soft. Her mouth fell open slightly, barely enough to exhale. Her heart and other vital organs were paralyzed. And still she didn't move.

"Are you going to run?" he whispered, staring at her lips.

Jenny's eyes were enormous, eating up her small face. "Can't," she said hoarsely. "It hurt too much last time."

"Oh, man." Tyler closed his eyes briefly, fighting himself for a moment. Every instinct within his soul told him to protect her, hold her, bring her closer. He wanted to soothe her war wounds with his lips, to smooth his hands over her hair, to somehow make everything all better for her. But she held her body stiffly, and the look on her face spoke more of uncertainty than passion.

Once again he put his own needs and wants second. Maybe it was second nature to him by now, who knew? But right now it was Jenny's well-being that came first, her comfort and her security. He'd failed to save her from being hurt before, but now he had a second chance. And so, though he wanted to kiss her more than he had ever wanted anything in his life, he contented himself with bringing his forehead softly against hers. Maybe it was the wild ride on the Harley that brought his emotions so close to the surface, but he actually felt a physical pain in his chest when he stemmed his urge.

"Does this bother you?" he asked. His palm was still on her cheek, his thumb lightly stroking the delicate skin below her eye. "Just...being this close?"

Jenny barely heard him. Her perceptions had suddenly narrowed until she took in only the faint smell of his cologne, the shape of his mouth, the faintest trace of stubble on his jaw. For a moment this odd child's bedroom felt potent with unspoken feelings and tantalizing isolation. It was all she could do to gather her thoughts enough to say, "I forgot the question."

"I think I did, too," he said dryly. He realized she was off balance, and perhaps closer than she thought to letting down her guard. This was bad. He could fight himself, but he couldn't fight both of them. He moved, or she might have, and suddenly he was standing again, talking to her as he backed toward the doorway. "Actually, I do want to talk to you about something, but it can wait till after dinner. Would you like me to send Rosie up and help you change?"

"I can manage," Jenny said, a little surprised by his abrupt withdrawal. And very relieved, she told herself. And a big fat liar. "What did you want to talk about?"

"It can wait," Tyler said, looking strangely guilty. "No big deal thing. Okay then, I'll come back up in a little while and help you downstairs. I thought it would be nice for you to get out of this Ringling Brothers room for a while. Rosie's got something cooking downstairs. Oh, and expect complete chaos, as well. Ella and the twins are here, too."

"I'll leave my wallet upstairs." She smiled faintly, looking small and battered and inexpressibly lovely. Her hair was a riot of color and curl, her full mouth looked like a silky rose, and her small hands held tightly to a sheep that might be a wolf. Or vice-versa.

"Oh, I'm a saint," Tyler muttered. "Just ask anybody."

And the reluctant saint took his leave with something akin to panic.

Five

Despite Jenny's protests that she could dress herself, Rosie came upstairs and helped her bathe and change into clean slacks and a cropped baby-blue tee. It took a bit of maneuvering to pull the khakis over Jenny's bandaged ankle, but they managed with a team effort. Rosie was completely down to earth, easy to be with and even easier to laugh with. Jenny felt an intangible tug on her emotions through it all, almost as if she had known Tyler's effervescent sister from before her accident. It seemed the most natural thing in the world to spend time with Rosie, not at all awkward or unnatural. Good old Rosie had also provided her with a couple of pain pills and a soft drink to wash them down, which eventually added a dazzling sparkle to Jenny's feeling of general well-being.

"You've got gorgeous hair," Rosie said wistfully, brushing out Jenny's long copper mane in front of the dresser mirror. "Mine is horrid, just baby-fine wisps that drive me crazy. It makes me look like I'm thirteen, I swear. And my poor boys have the same wretched hair."

Jenny was feeling awfully fine. Too fine, in fact, to practice much diplomacy. "So...they took after you more than your husband?"

Rosie snorted inelegantly. "No husband, just a *very* poor choice on my part. My mom died from cancer when I was only six, so I hardly remember having her around. When dad had his heart attack, I was a senior in high school. I took his death pretty hard. Tyler moved home to look after me and Ella, which certainly wasn't the life he had envisioned for himself. Anyway, I sort of got on the wrong track and ended up pregnant." She paused, then added quietly, "It wasn't the best of times for either of us. Poor Ty blamed himself, and ever since he has been way, *way* overprotective. The problem is, I'm twenty-three now and capable of looking after myself and my boys. They're finally in preschool and I've got a good job working at the county courthouse. I'm actually in control of my life, but try telling that to Tyler. I love him to bits, but when everyone in town knows that not only are you a mommy, but your brother is the sheriff, you spend a lot of weekends alone."

"But he has his job. Doesn't that keep him busy?"

Rosie shrugged. "Unfortunately, you're the most exciting thing that has happened to poor Sheriff Cook in years. This is Bridal Veil Falls, kiddo. It's depressing to admit, but we just don't have enough crime around here to keep things interesting for a guy like Tyler. He's had a fairly colorful past. He followed the rodeo circuit for quite a while before coming home to take care of me. He was amazing. He's been the World Champion All-Around Cowboy, the World Champion Bull Rider...there wasn't an animal he couldn't ride, I swear. He made more money than he could ever spend in his lifetime, but that wasn't why he did it. He loved the challenge.''

That explains the Brahma bulls, Jenny thought. The idea of Tyler Cook as a dusty cowboy with a number on his back was intensely appealing. ''Isn't that a dangerous way to make a living?''

''Yup,'' Rosie replied inelegantly. ''He was always on the injury report. But it never stopped him from winning. Never. He's always been hungry for everything life had to offer.''

''Something tells me I just may be the same way,'' Jenny replied. ''Sort of...restless. I don't think I'm used to staying in the same place for too long. But I won't know for sure until my little brain heals.''

Rosie smiled at Jenny in the mirror. ''It's probably best not to even worry about the amnesia. If it's anything like the movies, you'll see some little thing that sparks your memory and everything will come back to you. Till then, why fret?''

Jenny shrugged, busying herself picking invisible lint from her slacks. ''I hate to saddle your poor brother with an unwelcome house guest.''

Rosie grinned widely, looking for a moment exactly like her brother, right down to the fetching dimple. ''*Poor* Tyler? Honey, there's a huge difference between unexpected and unwelcome. I can promise you that you're a wonderful diversion for him. In fact, I asked him if I couldn't take you to my house, where you might be more at ease, and he told me—and I quote—'Not a chance in hell.' Now does that sound like a man being inconvenienced to you?''

Jenny smiled right back at her. She wasn't quite sure

what was so funny, but she started to chuckle. "Rosie, you're a really easy person to be around, do you know that? Your smile is just as contagious as your brother's smile. You know, I feel sort of bubbly, like my blood is carbonated. Really relaxed, though. *Incredibly relaxed.* Did I tell you that you're a very easy person to be around?"

"You did, yes," Rosie said with a mischievous glint in her blue eyes. "Tyler is going to have my head for this."

Jenny was listening to a happy buzz in her ears. "For what?"

"Nothing. Never mind. I'm going to call Sir Galahad now and have him carry you downstairs. You like spaghetti?"

"As far as I know," Jenny said happily, "I like everything. And everyone."

There was a merry-go-round in Jenny's head, dancing and glittering and whirling away. In some distant part of her mind, she knew she was riding a chemical high, and her emotions less than trustworthy. It didn't matter. She ate the most delicious spaghetti of her two-day life, drank the most delicious lemonade of her two-day life. Tyler was uncharacteristically quiet, watching her with alert, narrowed eyes. Almost as if he expected her to slip off her chair, Jenny thought with amusement. Silly man. Silly, funny, extremely good-looking man. He'd changed into a fresh white shirt and jeans, worn to white at the knees. His honey-brown hair was carelessly finger-combed back from his forehead and ears, almost long enough to cover his collar. He watched her and watched her all through dinner, but said very little. Now and then he would look over at his sister with murder in his electric-blue gaze, but on the whole he was pretty focused on Jenny.

Jenny, Ella, Rosie and the twins made up for Tyler's unusual silence. There was absolutely no awkward "barely know you" stage. The twin boys, Jamie and Justin, were fascinated by their new friend with the impressive bruises. They spent about two minutes eating and twenty minutes showing off, teaching Jenny a wonderful trick called "flying spoons." They demonstrated repeatedly, placing two spoons on the table, just so, then slamming their chubby little fists on one, which sent the other sailing through the air and into a full glass of water. The little guys were howling, Ella was attempting the trick with forks and Jenny was taking it all in with a slightly lopsided, beatific smile on her flushed face. Rosie's attention seemed more focused on her brother than her children, a curious expression in her eyes. Tyler didn't even seem to notice the many, many, many rules of table manners that were being broken by her irrepressible children. This was unusual for Tyler; he usually felt compelled to make the most of a teaching moment when it came to the twins. Apparently, he had more important things on his mind.

"I can talk like Donald Duck," Ella announced, giggling. Then, apparently forgetting what she'd just said: "Tyler? Aren't you the one who can talk like Donald Duck? Oh, that makes me just laugh and laugh."

"It's not me," Tyler muttered, twin spots of high color burning on his cheekbones. In truth, talking like Donald Duck had been one of the few things he'd excelled at during junior high. "Ella, you might not want to do that trick with forks. No, not with knives, either."

"It's pandemonium at Tyler Cook's house," Rosie

commented. "Jenny, things have been a lot livelier around here since you arrived. Not at all boring."

Again from Tyler, "Amen."

"Where was your home, dear?" Ella asked Jenny. "Before you came to live with Tyler?"

"I don't remember," Jenny told her kindly. She had long ago forgiven this bright-eyed woman-child for lifting her wallet. She realized how beautiful people got when they were older. Ella's lovely skin was so fine, so delicate, it seemed to shine with an inner luminosity. Her hair looked like a fluffy, pale cloud, and the smile lines in her face had been sweetly etched through the years. "I'm sure it will all come back to me, though."

Ella clapped her small hands in delight. "And that's exactly what I tell myself, as well. Thank goodness you're here, dear."

"Thank goodness you're here, too," Jenny said. She was still floating on a high cloud and completely at peace with the world. Ella was such a dear.

Tyler gave his sister a very stiff little smile. "Aren't we all so *cheerful* tonight? Especially Jenny. Rosie, have you any idea who might have been responsible for Jenny's *cheerfulness?*"

Rosie pulled a face at him. "Oh, lighten up. She was in pain, so I gave her some pills."

Tyler's jaw dropped. "Pills? Plural?"

"Two pills, sheriff," she scoffed. "I'm not a complete idiot. I was once, but I'm not now."

"Why didn't you wait until after she ate, Rosie?"

"Because she was in pain *before* we ate."

"Are you in pain, dear?" Ella asked Jenny. "My, you're brave. Not a word of complaint."

And so it went. Tyler was fairly composed for a man who was constantly worried that Jenny would slip beneath the table at any given moment. Spaghetti sauce decorated Jamie and Justin's faces by the time Rosie called a cease-fire to dinner. It was past eight, Rosie told her group. Time to head home and go nighty-night.

Jenny and Tyler stood on the front porch, waving at the departing guests like an old married couple. Jenny wasn't exactly giddy any longer; she was, however, extremely relaxed. She hadn't even minded when Tyler had carried her from the table to the front door. He was simply being a gentleman, one who smelled really nice. Even the thought that tonight she would be alone in the house with him didn't really bother her. Last night had gone swimmingly, right? They were both adults, and perfectly capable of handling the situation intelligently. She foresaw absolutely no problems. None. Zilch. Nix.

"Are you warm enough?" Tyler asked Jenny, still watching Rosie's car pull away from the curb. "We could go sit out back on the deck for a few minutes. A little fresh air might do you—might do us—a world of good. Yes?"

"Shertainly," Jenny said.

Tyler rolled his eyes and effortlessly scooped her up into his arms. She weighed nothing; she was a fragrant bundle of bruises, bandages and abrasions. He had an overwhelming urge to nuzzle her neck with his mouth, to work his way up to her lips and discover what it would be like to kiss this woman who constantly haunted his mind. But oh, no. *He* was the good guy, the one forever wearing the white hat and currently nursing a bad case of "poor me." He couldn't escape the feeling of being torn in two different directions. He wanted to be her caretaker, and he wanted to be her man, sweet and simple. How caveman-like was that? Every moment he spent with Jenny, whether she was starry-eyed medicated or not, was another twist on the old pressure valve. Her proximity to him made it all the harder to remember his good intentions. He had the sense of a time bomb ticking off, set in perfect rhythm to the meter of his hard-jumping heart.

"Hey!" Jenny said suddenly, in the tone of someone who had just discovered a cure to a terrible disease. "I remember something!"

Tyler's arms tightened around her, a sudden, burning heat curling in his belly. She remembered? *Not yet, not yet,* he thought. He wanted to be the only memory in her life for just a little while longer. He deliberately avoided looking down at her to hide the panic in his eyes. "What did you remember? Don't tell me—you really *are* Ophelia Detweiler."

Jenny looked up at him, her glazed eyes chiding. "Silly man. I meant I just remembered that you wanted to talk to me about something."

"Oh." Tyler let out a deep breath, telling his pulse to slow down. "Okay, that's all right. I mean, yes, I did want to talk to you. Where do you want to sit, madam? Lounger, chair or swing?"

Jenny realized he had already carried her all the way around the house. My, time was flying tonight. "Sure."

"Sure," Tyler muttered. "Okay. Madam wants to sit on her sure."

In the end they shared the white-fringed porch swing. It was padded with deep cushions, sinfully comfortable and just a fraction too small for two adults. Fortunately, Jenny was more the size of a child than an adult.

It was an evening identical to a thousand other summer evenings in Bridal Veil Falls. Soft, warm, sweet-smelling and peaceful. There had been so many times when Tyler had sat out here on the old back porch alone, feeling more restless than soothed by the eternal quiet. Somewhere in the world, there were new roads to explore, fascinating things to experience, mysterious challenges to meet. Though he had never regretted accepting responsibility for his family, he could never completely escape the sense that he was missing something vital in life.

But he didn't feel he was missing out on anything right now. There was a fiery-haired amnesiac rebel sharing his swing, a woman who hummed softly beneath her breath while staring up at the fat butterball moon in the sky. It took Tyler a moment to place the tune—"Starry, Starry Night."

His shoulder brushed softly against hers. He felt the brief contact as if it were something vaguely erotic, inexpressibly tantalizing. Jenny's profile was polished by the moonlight, adding an ethereal beauty that took him by the heart. Her lashes were star-tipped, as well, long and silky and ultrafeminine. In the shadows her bruises were muted, almost invisible. There was a bandage on her arm where she had had an IV in the hospital. For some reason that little flesh-colored bandage touched him as deeply as her beauty did. She was flesh and blood, regardless of how desperately she tried to be invulnerable. His protective instincts were hounding him, constantly pushing him to take a stand between Jenny and the rest of the world. John Wayne rides again.

He noticed her eyelids were growing heavy. "Jenny... if you're tired, we can call it a night. I shouldn't have kept you up this long. You're fresh from the hospital."

She waved her hand dismissively in the air, rejecting the suggestion. "I'm recovered, Sheriff. Really, I feel fine. And I had a wonderful time with your family. *Hey!*"

"Here we go again."

"You said you wanted to talk to me about something. I keep forgetting." Then, in a slightly different tone, "Did you find out something? About me, I mean."

Tyler stared at her expressionlessly. "Isn't that what we're hoping for?"

"Sure," she said. Then she tilted her head back against the cushion, staring at the stars. "That's what we're hoping for. Did you run a check on my Harley's plates or something?"

Tyler flushed. He knew damn well why he hadn't done that exact thing. Subconsciously he'd been putting it off. It was a clear dereliction of duty, and he wished he were ashamed of himself. Sadly, he was not. "I've been sort of preoccupied with everything that's gone on. I'll do that first thing Monday morning. Still, I might have found something that will help. When I picked up your duffel bag today, I went through it. I know I should have waited until you were with me, but I wondered if I might find some clue as to why you were riding a big, bad motorcycle through a strange little town all by yourself. It's kind of an unusual situation, especially for someone like you."

She raised her eyebrows. "Someone like me?"

"Well...a woman. A beautiful woman. A woman who looks more like she belongs in a limo than on a Harley. You're a puzzle, Jenny, a puzzle I can't solve."

She absorbed this quietly. Then she turned her head toward him, a tiny furrow etched between her brows and a faint smile on her lips. "And a pain in your neck?"

"Oh, no," Tyler whispered, matching her smile for

smile. "A surprise in my neck, maybe. A really nice surprise."

"Like having your house toilet papered on a Saturday night?"

"Oh, way better than that." They settled into a gentle silence, still looking, still smiling. Neither of them seemed to want to talk for the moment, and Tyler took the chance to drink her in. Tonight, tomorrow, it could all go away. She would turn and look at him and say, I remember. I remember my life, and you weren't part of it, were you?

But fanciful, dreamlike moments lived only for a short while; then reality intruded and facts had to be faced. Tyler forced himself to do just that, though he would have preferred to look at her till sunrise and not say a single word. "I did find a business card. There was no address book, no cell phone, no proof of reservations, nothing to indicate where you were going."

"Or where I came from," she replied softly.

Tyler had to force himself to continue. It wasn't easy, especially when he was so afraid this little tidbit could trigger her memory. "Actually, the business card had a California area code. You may have just been visiting there, you may live there. I don't know." He cleared his throat, but it didn't seem to ease the uncomfortable tightness there. "He may be a friend, he may be your lawyer."

Jenny was starting to feel a little cold. She wrapped her arms around herself, shivering. "A lawyer?"

"That's what the card said. Eliot Dearbourne, out of Los Angeles. Does that ring any bells?"

Jenny played that back in her mind. Eliot Dearbourne. An attorney from Los Angeles. Suddenly she became conscious of a sickening feeling in her stomach, and for the first time that evening, a headache started up. Eliot Dearbourne didn't ring any bells, but he didn't do her any good, either.

Eliot Dearbourne. There was something there, but she couldn't pin it down. Something less than pleasant, something her mind jumped away from like a red-hot stove.

"I don't want to think anymore tonight," she said abruptly, surprised at the panic in her own voice. "Okay? I just don't."

Tyler stared at her curiously. "I'm sorry. I was just trying to help."

She spoke quietly, urgently. "Then *help* me. Help me not to think."

The expression on her face shook him. She didn't look away from him, she didn't even blink. In the shadows her eyes were dark as midnight, shimmering with an intense, unreadable emotion. The cool night breeze was rife with confusing, conflicted feelings. It was a moment that could go either way—cautiously skirted or seized with blind hunger. The sort of moment that could change the course of someone's life.

"I can do that." He wasn't aware that he was speaking his thoughts aloud until he heard his own voice. That was when he knew he was through being a good boy.

She remained perfectly still, a silent storm in her dark eyes. Her gaze slowly slid down to his mouth, lingering there. Her own lips parted softly with a silent sigh. All around them shadows rustled in the moonlight, enclosing them in a rose-scented garden. For a moment time stood still...until Tyler gently framed her face with his hands, gently urging. They came together by inches, his hand slipping over the silky column of her hair. So soft, cool to the touch and exquisitely textured. His palm tingled and a sensual thrill shivered through his nerves. He brought a shining dark tendril of hair to his lips and kissed it, his eyes closing briefly. It was an innocent enough gesture, but the end result was a man whose thoughts were anything but innocent. What was left of his unimpressive self-control went up in flames.

Falling into the kiss was like falling into a surreal, graphic fantasy. For Tyler it was everything he had known it would be—her lips were softer than the touch of moonlight, parted and hotly responsive. He held her face in his hands and slanted his mouth to deepen his sensual assault, drinking fully with ravenous hunger. His mind urged gentleness in deference to her injuries. His body told him something else altogether: Now, now, while you still can. Taste her and touch her and remember it all.

He broke from the kiss, breathing hard and staring into Jenny's fire-bright eyes. Like Tyler she was gasping and her body trembled. Her palms were splayed against his chest, feeling the delicious warmth beneath. The night wind played gently through her hair, draping long, curling tendrils over his arms and shoulders, cocooning them together. He had been unprepared for the heavenly softness of her lips, the sweetness of her moist, silky flesh. There was so much to remember, so much to assimilate. He said nothing, just looked at her while he memorized every little thing—the light, rapid meter of her breath, the slightly swollen curves of shining lips, the way she stared right back at him with a dark confusion in her eyes.

He softly kissed her nose at the tip, unintentionally disturbing the waking dream. When Jenny blinked the world into focus and tucked her hands self-consciously in her lap, he took both of them in his, patiently untangling the knot of shaky fingers. Then his left hand spread open against her right, palm to palm. "Holding hands," he murmured softly, staring at their intertwined fingers. He didn't want her to be afraid of the magic they had made together. "Just like two little kids in grade school. You see? Very innocent."

Surprisingly, her mouth crooked in a small, shaky smile. "If this is how you acted in grade school, you should be ashamed of yourself."

He grinned, adopting a heavy Western twang. "Probably should, but I can't say as I am, ma'am."

A strange silence fell between them, taut with new rules and tantalizing mysteries. It was not so much awkward as it was surprising. Not since adolescence had Tyler suffered a loss of self-confidence when it came to women. The fact was, he'd simply never had time to be humble. He was always too busy running away from determined females who kept him looking over his shoulder like a deer during hunting season. But he was thinking hard and fast right now, desperately trying to come up with the right thing to say, the right thing to do. The more he thought, the further away the answers got. It had never mattered this much before. In fact, it had never mattered at all before.

"This is strange," he said finally. "You're the one who has amnesia—why am I the one suffering from brain cramps?"

Jenny attempted a little smile. "Maybe my ailment is contagious. Have you ever thought of that?"

"Maybe *you're* contagious."

She stifled a little yawn. Her euphoria had settled into a weightless, dreamy lethargy. "There's a scary thought. Poor Sheriff Cook. Saddled with contagious me."

She looked, Tyler thought suddenly, absolutely exhausted. What was he thinking, keeping her up this late? This woman had just survived an attack by a Pontiac. He stood up immediately, scooping Jenny into his arms with the ease of experience. It seemed he had been carrying this woman hither and yon since the first moment he'd met her. "Jenny, I loved kissing you and I'm going to kiss you again really soon, but not tonight. It's time for all good little amnesiacs to be in bed. Besides, having you anywhere near me is turning out to be damned masochistic while I'm responsible for your welfare."

"What about that lawyer person, Dearbourne?" Jenny asked, oddly reluctant to call it a night. "What should we do?"

"We'll worry about Dearbourne tomorrow." The shadows hid Tyler's guilty flush. "I probably should have called him today, but I was really busy doing…sheriff things. I barely had time to think. But tomorrow is Sunday, so we'll have plenty of time to get ahold of him. I can also run a check on the Harley if you'd like."

"If I *like*? Don't you want to get rid of me?"

Oh, if you only knew how much I don't want to get rid of you. "What I want isn't the question. And believe me, you're not ready to hear the answer yet." Tyler paused at the kitchen's slightly ajar back door to kick it open with his foot. "You'll just have to trust me on this one."

She was quiet for a minute, staring myopically at the small cleft in his stubborn chin. Up to his lashes, which were indecently long for a man and curled at the tips. His lips were also in her line of vision, and she had no choice but to stare at them, too. And remember what they had felt like on hers. Cowboy, she thought. Rugged, tough…sweet.

At that point a brazen spirit entered her body and took possession. This particular spirit was very bold, a hussy in fact, immediately planting a smacking kiss on Tyler's Cary Grant chin. The kiss was aimed at his mouth, but the brazen hussy could only reach his chin.

Her lovely face lifted up to Tyler like a flower to sunlight. A bright-eyed, brown-eyed Susan. He stood frozen in the doorway, looking down at her with comical disbelief. "What was that for?"

Her smile broke through the night shadows, impish and captivating and totally unrepentant. "I have no idea. Maybe *you're* contagious. Or I might have had too many pain pills and too much wine with dinner. Or maybe a combination of all of the above."

"It's a distinct possibility," he said flatly, sensual urgency singing bright notes in his blood. Wasn't this the damnedest thing? Here he was holding an alluring, albeit overly medicated woman in his arms, figuring out how to take her to bed while *not* taking her to bed. "You don't make this easy, Jenny. I'm trying to be a gentleman."

"Am I making it difficult?"

"Yes."

"Well, I'm sorry, then. Truly. It's just that...I have this feeling..." Her wistful voice trailed off into silence. Her expression was pensive, almost bewildered.

"A feeling...?" Tyler prompted.

Softly she said, "That this night is a dream, a fantasy. That nothing matters right now, because somehow tomorrow everything will be very real and very different. Do you understand?"

"I wish I didn't," he said quietly. He dropped his chin, his face nestled in her hair. "Sweet girl...I wish I didn't."

Six

As Tyler stood under the shower Sunday morning, he deliberately turned the water temperature to heart-attack cold. He was trying to wake up, which wasn't easy. He'd been wide-eyed and restless most of the night, creeping around his bedroom like a reverent little church mouse, afraid if he made the slightest noise he might wake Jenny up. She needed her rest. Finally, around 6:00 a.m. he'd dozed off. One hour later his alarm went off and he'd fallen out of his bed trying to kill the thing before the shrill buzzing disturbed his beautiful guest. On Sunday mornings he usually got up early to work in his yard and wash his car. Suburban Sundays, he called them, often wishing he had something more exciting to do.

He'd never suffered from insomnia before, but he wasn't surprised. Since meeting Jenny, there had been a lot of brand-new experiences in his life. It was his first time arresting a woman in a Mexican restaurant. First time stealing bowling shoes. First time terrorizing an entire hospital, not to mention his best friend Grady. First time riding a Harley straight through the middle of town at close to 130 miles an hour. *Awesome.* When he was on that machine, he'd wanted to head for the stars, to feel the wind whipping his face and the summer sun heating his back. He'd wanted to give in to each and every tantalizing, self-gratifying urge he had, just like in the old days. But more than anything, he wanted to do it all with a copper-haired adventuress nestled behind him, her arms looped around his waist. He wanted to share the ride.

Still, it hadn't all been a rush. Other firsts had been as enjoyable as a root canal. It was the first time he had carried a woman to bed, tucked her in and, at her bright-eyed insistence, read from an old, dog-eared copy of *Reader's Digest* until she started snoring. She had a really cute snore, high-pitched and almost soundless. He couldn't leave the room for a full ten minutes; he stood beside her bed with his hands pushed safely in his pockets and lusted for all he was worth. Snore, lust, snore, lust. He no longer knew what to expect from himself anymore. A chaste little bedtime story after their soul-searing kiss had been almost more than he could handle. Had Jenny been completely lucid, she would have noticed the beads of sweat gathering on his brow.

Even as he shivered under the cold water, he felt fire shooting right through him as he replayed the events of the night before. Prior to meeting Jenny, a kiss had never had that effect on him. A woman had never had that effect on him. And Lord knew a criminal had never had that effect on him. He'd been powerfully drawn to her from the moment they met, despite the highly unusual circumstances. And ever since then, he'd fallen deeper and deeper every time he looked in her warm-brandy eyes. The thought of ever saying goodbye to her was anathema to him.

Downstairs on the front hall table was a little white business card with a number he didn't want to call. He'd also told Jenny he would run the Harley's plates, which would almost certainly result in a wealth of information he wasn't sure he wanted. But what choice did he have? He had no more excuses. At some point he needed to remember who he was and what his professional obligations were.

A heavy cloud of foreboding settled over him, playing with sickening fingers in his middle. He couldn't ignore the facts, much as he would like to do just that. The woman he had met in Enchilada Ernie's had been a defensive, prickly soul, wary of everything and suspicious of everyone. Tyler had been around enough to know that kind of reaction was usually the result of hard lessons learned from a less than wonderful past. But since he'd brought Jenny to his home, she'd allowed herself to relax somewhat, showing fascinating glimpses of an endearing, almost childlike soul. Part of that sparkling innocence was no doubt due to the pain medication, but underneath he caught a glimpse of a woman who was gifted with a warmly affectionate personality and a delightful, spontaneous sense of humor. Last night Jenny had been generous with her smiles, teasing with him, allowing him to get physically close to her without turning into a cactus and resorting to defensive, verbal jousting. Maybe he was being too much of an optimist, but he truly believed that behind her guarded walls, she was very, very human. Her shell was only skin deep. He would have bet his life on it.

Still, with Jenny he never knew what to expect from

moment to moment. A faint smile curled up the edges of his lips as he wondered who she would be today.

Jenny wasn't feeling very confident today.

The problem was, she remembered absolutely everything about the night before. At the time, lost in a lovely cloud of fine medication and fine wine, her behavior had seemed perfectly logical. But in the harsh light of morning, it felt more humiliating than logical. And what about making Tyler read the bedtime story? *Geez,* that had been utterly ridiculous. At the time she was just searching for reasons to make him stay with her. She'd been so relaxed and so content with the moment. She was beginning to wonder if she'd had much happiness in her life before finding herself in Bridal Veil Falls. Last night's blissful contentment had felt so alien, yet so wonderful.

Still, one thing hadn't changed with the dawn of a new day. Last night she had allowed herself to open up to Tyler, dropping her defensive attitude for a while and just enjoying his company. That had created a new intimacy that stayed with her. She couldn't pretend that nothing had changed, much as she would like to. Something definitely had changed. Whatever had led her to lower her defenses couldn't be reversed. It might have been wise and prudent to keep him at arm's length, but it was a little too late for wisdom and prudence. To further complicate matters, she had the ominous sensation of impending change, as if she knew her memory was building on the horizon like a particularly nasty storm cloud. And when it all came back to her, when she remembered the whos and whats and whys of her past, it wasn't going to be a relief. She knew that with a cold, flat certainty. She couldn't escape the unsettling fear that whoever she was, it wasn't who she wanted to be.

In short, she was in a pickle. She was in a whole barrel of pickles.

On the bright side, her ankle was feeling much better. She no longer needed pain medication, which gave a new clarity to her thoughts and feelings. Feeling oddly sensitive, she hobbled downstairs to meet Tyler for breakfast, hardly needing the single crutch she used. Her unique outfit had been a gift from the woman she had been before being hit by a Pontiac. She was dressed in low-slung hip-huggers and one of the four shirts she found in her duffel bag, a lightweight, cropped lavender sweater that revealed Jenny's rather large, diamond-studded belly-button ring. She wasn't sure if the diamond was real or not, but it certainly looked it. She decided there was something sort of catchy about her unique Gypsy flair—the silver hoops dangling from her ears, the men's watch on her wrist inlaid with chunky turquoise stones, the eye-catching color of her toenail polish. The financial wisdom of investing heavily in a belly-button ring, however, was seriously debatable. At least she was an *original* amnesiac. There certainly weren't many people who could say that.

Tyler was seated at the kitchen table, reading the Sunday paper and basking in a hazy square of June sunshine. He had dressed down for his lazy day at home, wearing threadbare jeans and a simple T-shirt, white cotton printed with the faded slogan: Java-enabled. Jenny smiled when she saw his feet were bare, toes wiggling and reveling in freedom. She was witnessing the sheriff's day off.

"Good morning," she said, feeling suddenly shy. She kept having flashbacks of the night before, very graphic flashbacks that made it a little difficult to concentrate. "I made it downstairs in one piece." She smiled and shrugged. "Crutch-enabled, but I'm making good progress."

Tyler stood up immediately, which Jenny thought was actually kind of sweet. Standing up when a woman entered a room was a rarely seen expression of old-fashioned chivalry. A bright Sunday morning looked good on him. The bay window in the kitchen faced east, and the morning sun was playing with his layered, rainbow-brown hair. He looked endearingly earnest and guilt-ridden. "I should be shot. I was coming up to help you, I really was. I just thought you might need some time to fix yourself..." He rolled his eyes. "I am the soul of tact."

"To fix what?" Jenny prompted, fighting a smile. "To fix myself up a little?"

"Well, women seem to...oh, hell. I was not implying you need to *do* anything with yourself. I mean, of all the women in the world who do not need any fixing up whatsoever, you are the most...look, we're going to start over." He smiled grimly, pulling out a chair for her. "Good morning, Jenny. Sit, please. Would you like coffee?"

Jenny's eyes sparkled. "I'm sure I use lipstick and mascara and perfume like everyone else. And good morning to..." Her voice trailed off. Without warning, she had a hazy, surreal memory of seeing her own reflection in a mirror, dabbing on some lip gloss and hastily combing her damp mane of hair with her fingers. She could even see the details of the mirror itself, the antique-white oval frame and a tiny chip in the glass near the bottom. That particular mirror was not hanging in the bathroom upstairs. Which meant it was somewhere else. Somewhere she had been *before*.

The utter blankness of unclothed fear flooded her dark, expressive eyes. She knew if she focused and concentrated, she would see something more than just a white-framed mirror. She was certain of it. More details, more clues that would eventually lead her to the answers she lacked. But where there should have been excitement, inexplicable panic reigned. Jenny literally felt the hairs on the back of her neck rise up.

"Tyler!" To her rather limited knowledge, she had never let loose with a hysterical war whoop. But that was exactly what it sounded like. She lost the crutch and grabbed for Tyler's shoulders, her fingers digging into the hard muscles. It was all out there in a murky mist, the answers, the fear, the absolute terror. But before Jenny could steel herself to try and remember, a stabbing pain hit her at the base of her skull with all the force of a heavy blow. It was so violent, so unexpected that she lost color in her face as if someone had pulled a plug in her heel.

"What?" Acting on experience, Tyler instinctively swept her off the floor and into his arms. Again. It seemed as if he had been carrying this woman around since the first time he'd arrested her. He was so shocked, so taken by surprise, he actually found himself in danger of hyperventilating. Never in his life had he seen a complexion the color of cream cheese, but Jenny's was pretty close. "Jenny, tell me. Your ankle? Your head? Are you sick? Your heart? Good Lord, are you having a heart attack?"

"Not my *heart*," Jenny groaned, gathering her wits about her enough to send him an exasperated look.

"What do you mean, am I having a heart attack? Do I look like I'm having a heart attack?"

His mind spinning, Tyler defended his diagnosis. "Why not? It's the only thing that hasn't happened to you yet."

"It's my *head*. This pain suddenly hit me...I was starting to remember something, and this terrible pain hit me. Could you put me down somewhere? I can't breathe."

Tyler realized he was at fault for her lack of oxygen. He was holding her close to his chest with all the strength in his body, and that was considerable. He forced himself to relax a bit, trying on a calm, reassuring smile. It didn't fit. "I'm going to put you in a chair, all right? Can you sit up?"

Jenny was holding her head with both hands, and barely heard him. "Whatever. It's easing up, I think. It was so bad, I couldn't see for a minute. It even hurts to think...."

Tyler gently settled her in a chair, going down on his haunches beside her and murmuring reassuring words as his mind raced. A particularly nasty thought had penetrated his panic. It occurred to him that Jenny's symptoms might be something completely unrelated to her accident. Perhaps she was ill, gravely ill. What if she needed some sort of medication? What if his reluctance to put an end to her dependence on him had put her life in danger? For the second time that day, he said, "I should be shot." But this time he truly meant it.

"It wasn't your fault," Jenny said faintly, misunderstanding. "I guess...maybe I need to rest for a little while. Do you mind?"

Tyler didn't mind at all. He had business to tend to, and he couldn't begin until he was sure Jenny was safe in bed. He helped her upstairs, promising to bring her some breakfast in a few minutes. He had a few calls to make, he told her, which was the truth. Police business, which was a lie.

Downstairs again, Tyler grabbed the business card on the table in the hall, then went to the telephone on the kitchen wall. There were two numbers, one listed as Eliot Dearbourne's office, one his cell phone. Tyler wasn't particularly fond of lawyers as a species, but was willing to give Dearbourne the benefit of the doubt for Jenny's sake. He punched in the cell phone number listed, and heard a carefully recorded, well-modulated voice making his excuses: "You've reached the mobile number of Eliot Dearbourne, Attorney at Law. Your call is very important to me, so please leave your message at the tone. Thank you so much and have a good day."

Like you care if I have a good day, Tyler thought, then left a clipped message. "My name is Tyler Cook and I'm the sheriff of Bridal Veil Falls in Montana. A woman you may know, Jenny Kyle, has had an accident within my jurisdiction. It's vital that you get in touch with me. *Vital.* Please return my call immediately." He then left his home phone, his office number, his cell number and, as an added precaution, Rosie's number. He called the man's office and left the same message there. He wasn't taking any chances. He then called in the Harley's plates and was told the motorcycle was registered to Jennifer Maria Kyle, with a California address and license. Tyler caught himself letting out a breath he hadn't realized he'd been holding. A part of him had been afraid the Harley would turn out to be registered to a man. A boyfriend…or husband.

The Los Angeles police promised to look into the matter and call Tyler when they found out anything. It shouldn't be long.

There was nothing left he could do. His little game of postponing the moment of truth had been stupid, an idiotic risk to take just because she was...

Becoming necessary. Like oxygen.

Tyler hated the feeling of being powerless. Throughout his childhood he'd been powerless when it came to earning his father's approval. He'd been powerless to prevent his father's death and, despite his best efforts, powerless to help his troubled teenage sister when he'd come home. Fortunately in the following years, the situation with his home and family had greatly improved. His own desire to earn some sort of absolution, however, remained in the back of his mind. It was too late to make peace with his father, but it wasn't too late to do the right thing for Jenny.

As he was standing in the kitchen staring off into space, pondering his next move, the phone rang. He jumped on it as if it were a fire alarm. "Yes?"

"'Yes?'" Grady's surprised voice said. "That's how you answer the phone these days? You're an uncouth cowboy, Cook."

"Jenny has a headache," Tyler snapped. "In fact, I was just about to call you and tell you."

After a short pause he said, "A headache. Thank you for letting me know. As her doctor, I should keep up on these things."

"Damn it, Grady, this is a *bad* headache. It came on very suddenly, like someone had conked her on the back of her head."

"Tyler," Grady said in a long-suffering voice, "I thought we had a talk about this. Jenny needs time to heal. It's not going to be an overnight process. In plain

English, she'll feel icky for a while. Do you understand?''

Tyler wasn't in the mood to be sensible. Or even polite. "Icky? Your professionalism astounds me.''

There was a long silence, enough time for Grady to count to ten. "Yes. You'd be surprised how professional I can be. Over the years I've had a great deal of experience dealing with hysterical friends and relatives of the patient. In this case, that would be you.''

Tyler knew he was somewhat hysterical—in a controlled, manly way, of course. So he didn't argue the point. "Grady, shut your pie hole and listen to me here. Something's wrong. Jenny was feeling much better, she was even starting to remember things. Then suddenly this pain hits her, right out of the blue. It didn't seem to last long, but…what if this problem isn't even related to the accident? What if she has some kind of medical condition we don't even know about? She couldn't tell us about it because she doesn't remember anything yet.''

There must have been something in Tyler's voice that persuaded Grady to take his friend seriously. "That's possible, I suppose, but what are the chances of that happening? I just can't see it. You say she was beginning to remember things? And that's when she suddenly got this headache?''

"Yes.'' Tyler shoved his hand through his hair, pacing a small track back and forth in front of the wall phone as if he were keeping guard. "I don't know if that's coincidence or if it means something. Hell, at this point I don't know anything.''

"Have you ever thought she might not want to remember?'' Grady asked thoughtfully. "That this is her body telling her mind to back off? I mean, it's a wild guess, but it would make a weird kind of sense.''

Tyler's skin felt chilled. His heartbeat became hard and uneven. "Are you kidding me? You mean, there's something more painful for her to deal with than the amnesia?"

"Don't panic. I'm just throwing out ideas here. Look, if her headache gets worse, take her right to the emergency room. And if she seems really confused—"

"*Confused?* Grady, she can't remember anything! How much more confused could she be?"

"Will you stop with the guard-dog thing and listen to me? Don't leave her alone. Watch for any changes in her behavior. And for the time being, I think it might be prudent not to encourage her to think about her past. Distract her. I'm sure you can figure out ways to distract her." Then, curiously, "Have you found out anything about her people yet, where she might live? They might be able to help us understand what's going on here."

"I'm working on it. Thanks, Grady. This means...she means..."

"Are you trying to tell me you care about her? Ty, I've known that since the night you brought her into the hospital. You looked worse than she did. Look, I know it's important to you to look out for her, but there's really nothing more you can do. For what it's worth, one thing I've learned practicing medicine is that the worst-case scenario seldom materializes. Try to remember that."

Tyler smiled faintly, grateful for his old friend's concern. He could have expressed his gratitude with a heartfelt speech, but Grady would have thought he'd had a mental breakdown. "Won't it be wonderful when you stop *practicing* medicine and start being a real doctor?"

"Have you any idea how many times I've heard that stupid joke? It's one of the drawbacks of practicing—of *dispensing* my medical expertise in the same town where I grew up. I get absolutely no respect. Call me if you need me today, all right? If I'm not home, my service can reach me. Good luck, buddy."

Jenny was sitting up in bed when Tyler came upstairs bearing a breakfast tray. She was idly rummaging through a stack of reading material she'd pulled off the bedside table. Comic books. Coloring books. And one glossy magazine that seized her attention in the same way a sudden earthquake might have.

"It's you," Jenny said stupidly, jabbing her finger at the cover. "Ohmigosh, it's *you*."

Tyler glanced at the cover of *American Cowboy* and shrugged. "Oh. That."

"Yes, *that*." Jenny couldn't take her eyes off the sunlit face on the magazine. Sheriff Tyler Cook, looking for all the world like some fantasy out of the Old West. He was gorgeous, too gorgeous to be an actual walking, talking, horse-straddling, bull-riding, money-winning cowboy, but who said life was fair? His dusty beige hat was pushed back on his head, his summer-blue eyes sparkling wickedly beneath the tangled fringe of sweat-darkened hair across his forehead. The pure and simple joy of his wide grin stole the breath from her lungs. Whatever he'd been doing when that photograph was taken had obviously been something he'd gotten quite a kick out of. The caption was simple: Rodeo's Tyler Cook—Next Best Thing To Superman. "This is a national publication! You never told me you were famous."

"I wasn't famous," Tyler said carelessly. "Not unless you were a member of the PRCA that year. I'm famous now, though—best and only sheriff in Bridal Veil Falls.

Play the
"LAS VEGAS"
GAME
GET 3 FREE GIFTS!
FREE GIFTS!
FREE GIFTS!
FREE GIFTS!
TURN THE PAGE TO PLAY!
Details inside!

Play the "LAS VEGAS" Game
and get
3 FREE GIFTS!

FREE GIFTS!

FREE GIFTS!

1. Pull back all 3 tabs on the card at right. Then check the claim chart to see what we have for you — 2 FREE BOOKS and a gift — ALL YOURS! ALL FREE!

2. Send back this card and you'll receive brand-new Silhouette Desire® novels. These books have a cover price of $4.25 each in the U.S. and $4.99 each in Canada, but they are yours to keep absolutely free.

3. There's no catch. You're under no obligation to buy anything. We charge nothing — ZERO — for your first shipment. And you don't have to make any minimum number of purchases — not even one!

4. The fact is, thousands of readers enjoy receiving their books by mail from the Silhouette Reader Service™. They enjoy the convenience of home delivery...they like getting the best new novels at discount prices, BEFORE they're available in stores...and they love their *Heart to Heart* newsletter featuring author news, horoscopes, recipes, book reviews and much more!

5. We hope that after receiving your free books you'll want to remain a subscriber. But the choice is yours — to continue or cancel, any time at all! So why not take us up on our invitation, with no risk of any kind. You'll be glad you did!

Visit us online at
www.eHarlequin.com

FREE!
No Obligation to Buy!
No Purchase Necessary!

Play the "LAS VEGAS" Game

PEEL BACK HERE ▶
PEEL BACK HERE ▶
PEEL BACK HERE ▶

YES! I have pulled back the 3 tabs. Please send me all the free Silhouette Desire® books and the gift for which I qualify. I understand that I am under no obligation to purchase any books, as explained on the back and opposite page.

326 SDL DNX5   225 SDL DNYC

FIRST NAME	LAST NAME

ADDRESS

APT.#	CITY

STATE/PROV.	ZIP/POSTAL CODE

(S-DA-09/02)

7	7	7	**GET 2 FREE BOOKS & A FREE MYSTERY GIFT!**
❀	❀	❀	**GET 2 FREE BOOKS!**
🍒	🍒	🍒	**GET 1 FREE BOOK!**
🔔	🔔	🔔	**TRY AGAIN!**

Offer limited to one per household and not valid to current Silhouette Desire® subscribers. All orders subject to approval.

Sit back, I've got some food here for you. You like hash browns?''

For once Jenny did as she was told. She had something to focus on besides her own woes. This was wonderful. "What's the PRCA?"

Tyler set the tray on her lap. It was actually a cookie sheet—the bachelor's answer to a lap tray. "Professional Rodeo Cowboy's Association. I ate dirt for a living. How are you feeling?"

"Better," Jenny said. "The headache eased up. Tell me about rodeos."

"Will you eat while I talk?"

Jenny looked at the omelette, fruit and hash browns that the American Cowboy had cooked up for her. "Somehow," she promised, "I'll manage."

And so, because he cared about her and he wanted to distract her, he sat on the edge of the bed and told her about rodeos.

Fortunately, Jenny could chew while she listened. She smiled when he told her about his start in rodeos—riding one of his dad's calves when he was two years old. By the time he was twelve years old, he'd made it to the national finals of the Little Britches Rodeo, which whet his appetite for lights, dirt, wild crowds and wilder stock. He talked about his sport in an offhand way that belied the pain, determination and awesome talent it must have taken him to achieve the standing of All-Around World Champion. But his expressive eyes lit up, and his quiet voice warmed to his subject, and Jenny knew he had loved his moment in the sun.

"How do you stay here?" she heard herself ask quietly. Her food had disappeared long ago, along with her headache. The empty, bachelor's lap tray had been moved to the floor. "All that excitement, all the noto-riety...don't things ever get too quiet here for you?"

Tyler shrugged. He was sitting next to Jenny on the bed, his back leaning against the wall. "I don't really think about it much. Rosie, Ella, the terrible two...they mean more to me than a gold belt buckle ever could. There are a lot of times I wish I'd made different choices. I was gone when my dad died. I was gone when Rosie started having problems. Granted, the money helped my family out, but I'm not sure it made up for my absence here. It was kind of a Catch-22. No matter how much I won...I felt like I couldn't really win."

Rosie looked down at the magazine again. "You look happy. Tyler, there's nothing wrong with following your own star, finding your own way in life."

He smiled faintly. "That's what I used to tell myself. I was caught up with doing my own thing, perfectly willing to trade a few broken bones for the approval and the money and the challenge. But now...I'm not sure it was worth the price other people paid."

"But you did what you needed to do, right? What you wanted to do?"

"Oh, I've always pretty much gone after what I wanted." And here she was, her curly head leaning against his shoulder. *What he wanted.*

After a long moment Jenny said softly, "You're a good man."

He cocked one eyebrow at her. "You've been at the pain pills again, haven't you?"

"Nope." She grinned up at him. "Just speaking my mind. Fortunately, I'm a woman and allowed to change it."

So sweet, so earnest, a smile curling her beautiful Bambi eyes. Because it seemed perfect, the most natural thing in the world, he leaned down and kissed her mouth softly. It was the briefest contact, a mere butterfly kiss, but carried seriously high voltage.

"Maybe you could try and remember that," he whispered against her parted lips.

"The kiss?"

"The man." One more kiss, lingering a fraction of a second longer than the first. "Not the cowboy, just...the man."

Jenny had no idea if she was a forward woman by nature. She rather doubted it, which made it even more surprising when she lifted her hand, cradling the hard curve of his cheek. Her thumb stroked his cheekbone softly. He hadn't shaved yet that morning—she could feel the scratchy-soft beard against her palm. His forehead dipped against hers, his brow furrowed, his eyes drifting closed. "What are you doing?" Jenny whispered. "You look so serious."

"I'm memorizing." He opened his eyes then, the sensual, fierce flash of electric blue catching Jenny by the throat. "Memories are roses in winter, did you know that? Something to hold on to when things get a little cold."

"I've never heard that." She gave him a wobbly smile, intensely aware of his physical warmth, his broad shoulders and hard chest. Everything that made him different from her was etched in her mind with fire. "At least, I don't think I've ever heard that. You're sort of a cowboy poet, aren't you?"

"Not hardly." But his voice was distracted, his eyes focused intently on her lips. So soft, so ripe and full, the little edges curled upward like ribbon. They belonged in a scandalous movie, those lips. He couldn't help it—he lowered his head with a sudden hunger, catching her mouth beneath his. Some far corner of his mind registered the fact that she met him halfway, which only added fuel to the fire. He wasn't the only one who wanted.

Tyler's body sang, instantly aroused. His lips tasted, held, broke and kissed again. Her hands tangled in his hair, holding him close. She parted her mouth with complete surrender. *Now she cooperates,* Tyler thought with something akin to panic. *Now, when we're both on this bed and I'm half out of my mind with need.*

Without being conscious of it happening, they slid down on the bed, legs tangling together on the disheveled bed sheets. Never once did Tyler stop kissing her, on her lips, her neck, her hair, her lips again. The more he had, the more he wanted. He tried to be gentle, but it took a superhuman effort. He'd waited all his life for her. He had a lot of lost time to make up for.

"Jenny..." Flushed, he broke from the kiss, holding her beautiful, heart-shaped face in his shaking fingers. "You're injured. I don't want to hurt you..."

"Then don't stop," Jenny whispered. "This is so strange, but...suddenly it feels so good to be held. So good. Just hold me, Tyler. Please."

She had no idea what she was asking of him. *Just* holding her, in fact, was impossible. But Tyler tempered himself as much as he could, easing the iron band of his arms, trailing gentle kisses down the lovely line of her throat. He pressed his lips against the pulse that jumped there, tasting the rhythm of her heartbeat. Hectic, fevered...matching his exactly.

"You're all right?" he murmured, worrying even as his hands slipped down her shoulders, his fingers brushing the sides of her breasts over the cashmere sweater. The slight contact left him dizzy, and he tried to remember he was the caretaker here, the one responsible for her welfare. He knew she was confused, constantly navigating her way. He didn't want to add to that stress, but he simply didn't have the willpower to change the course of the river rippling through him. Desire had never come like this before, hot and fierce and as untamed as any wild animal he had ever faced. Desire had always been easily contained, *civilized.*

He didn't feel civilized now.

"You…" Jenny gasped when his hands molded the curves of her breasts, "You worry too much about me. This feels…I feel…"

Tyler pressed a shaky smile against her neck. "Me, too."

Jenny wondered if this was all as new to her as it felt. Being held by someone, focusing on their breath, their body, the look in their eyes…in a strange way it was both comforting and arousing. Little by little her walls came down, a part of her relaxing that had been tense since Enchilada Ernie's. She pulled back her head slightly, permitting herself one long, delicious look at her American cowboy. She loved his hair. It seemed to always be a bit disheveled, tangling in straight lengths on his neck and forehead. That hair gave a touch of the little boy to him, a sharp contrast to the knowing sensual heat in his heavy-lidded, hypnotic eyes. He had magic.

"Do you want to know a secret?" she whispered, her lips quirking at one corner.

It took Tyler two tries to make his voice work. And when it finally did, it sounded like sandpaper, gritty with strain and tight with the emotions that shivered between them. "I love secrets. Tell me."

"I'm tired of thinking," she said, her dark chocolate

eyes round and solemn. "I don't want to think anymore. I want to feel."

Tyler wondered how much one man could take before he snapped. Briefly he closed his eyes while he tried to gather his thoughts and discipline his body, but all he saw was Jenny. He opened his eyes, and all he saw was Jenny. He had a feeling that had she been halfway around the world from him, he would still see her face everywhere he looked. "You don't know what you're doing to me," he said. "You don't know."

"I'll tell you what you're doing to me," Jenny replied softly. She took his hand in hers, placing it directly over her heart. Her smile was enchanting, surrounding him with a warm, physical presence. "Do you feel that? That's my Tyler-rhythm. Crazy, hectic, out of control."

Tyler lost pace with his breath. "Is this a truce or a surrender?"

"I don't know," she said honestly. The edges of her moist lips curled like a cat's tail, enchanting him. "I'm so tired of *thinking*. When I look at you, when I see that look in your eyes...I feel precious. And I want to give back everything you're giving me, the rush, the sweetness, the feeling of belonging. Could I do that, do you think? Can a girl with no memory of her experience affect a man like you?"

Tyler smiled faintly, remembering his very recent sleepless nights. She probably had no idea how good she looked to him, her riotous, curling hair reflecting light in every strand, her Bambi eyes beguiling. "You pack quite a wallop, little girl. I've been hit hard by a lot of things in my life, but never by anything like you." He closed the distance between them slowly, watching his own reflection in her round-eyed stare. His open mouth took hers gently, probing, stroking the swollen warmth of her lips. After this kiss, he thought, she would know. She would understand what she meant to him.

Tyler had never kissed a woman like this in his life. His dreams had become wishes, and his wishes had come true. She was like an exotic delicacy to him, fragrant and mysterious and addictive. His fingers were tangled in her hair, and he could feel them trembling. He gave his heart in his kiss, imprinting on her mouth all the intense, erotic feelings that had been torturing him since the first time he'd seen her. He held nothing back. Somewhere in the back of his mind he heard the soft sound she made deep in her throat, like a whimper. A new recklessness seized him as he tasted the warmth and fire of her mouth. He deepened the kiss, taking it from sweet to savage in the space of a heartbeat. It wasn't a conscious choice; his body knew it was the next step. Losing control.

He rolled onto his back, pulling her with him, spreading her over him. He tried to be gentle, mindful of his accident-prone love's bruises, but it was more difficult than he ever could have imagined. Little by little they sank deeper into the moment, and Tyler felt as if there had never been a woman before Jenny. Like her, he was born yesterday. Or actually, the day before.

Gasping, Jenny pulled back her head, staring down at him. "It comes so fast between us...all the feelings."

"That's because they've been there since the first day," Tyler said hoarsely, drinking her in with his hot blue eyes. "At least for me they have."

She gave him a shaky-sweet smile. "You couldn't stand me."

"Wrong."

"You arrested me."

"Right." This time he rolled her on her back, being

careful not to jar her ankle. Looking down at the beautiful creation of his desire, he dropped a soft, lingering kiss on her mouth. "And if I have to keep arresting you every day for...oh, hell."

Jenny stilled. "Oh, hell, what? What's wrong?"

"Rosie," Tyler grated out. "*She's* what's wrong. Did you just hear that coughing noise in the driveway?"

"I didn't hear anything," Jenny said. "I was preoccupied."

Tyler steeled himself for a next-to-impossible effort. Gently he rolled over on his side, then sat up on the bed. The hollow aching in the pit of his abdomen had spread lower—tight and burning. He felt like a time bomb ready to detonate. Until now, he hadn't realized he had homicidal tendencies. "Jenny, that coughing noise comes from my sister's beloved station wagon. She's here."

As if to confirm his words, Jenny heard the front door slam. "Why is she here?"

"Because she's nosy," Tyler grated out. "She *never* visited me this much before I met you, I'll tell you that. I was the one always checking on her." He stood up, facing the doorway, hands planted on his hips. And he talked to himself. "I am going to go stark raving mad. One man can't take all this stress. If she's brought the terrible two, I won't be responsible for my actions. I don't *care* if she's my sister. Jenny?"

"What?" she asked, bereft and shell-shocked on the bed.

He turned on his heel, holding out a hand. "Let's run away."

For a moment there was no expression at all on her passion-flushed face. Then a slow, honeyed smile spread over her lips and she put her hand in his. "I like the way you think."

Seven

Tyler kept a Jeep in the garage, a nice change from riding around in his boat-size policemobile. The rag top was off and he left it that way, buckling Jenny in as if she were the most precious piece of fine china in the world. Nothing more could happen to her, he told himself. Nothing bad, never again.

They headed west, skirting main street and leaving Bride Falls on Her Head behind. Jenny wore one of Tyler's ball caps to keep her hair from whipping her in the face. There was a blanket and a thermos of coffee in the back. Despite the sensual tension that shivered between them, the mood was light and funny, as if they had indeed run away from home. They'd left Rosie fixing lunch for herself and the twins back at Tyler's house. And other than Rosie cocking her eyebrow at the hickey blooming on Jenny's neck, no questions were asked.

"Where are we going?" Jenny shouted, to be heard over the wind.

Tyler grinned at her, looking for the moment very much like a certain heartthrob on the cover of *American Cowboy*. "*Away*. Is that good enough?"

Jenny realized it had been some time since she had been able to look at him without the rhythm of her pulse changing radically. Still, it was probably understandable, considering that Tyler had been blessed with far more than his fair share of charm and looks. "Better than good enough."

They both seemed to be in the same mood—deliberately lighthearted and unwilling to talk about anything remotely serious. They cranked the Jeep's CD player up as loud as it would go, Tyler singing along with Brooks and Dunn and Martina McBride. Jenny didn't know the words to the songs, but she clapped enthusiastically for her chauffeur after each performance. The emotional tensions of the past few days seemed to slowly melt away, out of sight and out of mind.

The naked physical tension was something else. It was constantly there between them, chattering, digging, needling. It kept Jenny quite literally on the edge of her seat, while Tyler gripped the steering wheel with white-knuckled hands. They sang, they laughed...and they darted simmering, longing looks when the other wasn't watching. Nothing had changed since those few minutes in the bedroom. Tyler carried his need with him in the pit of his belly, while Jenny's cheeks remained permanently flushed and her imagination wandered. Something was going to happen, she knew. Soon. It was almost a relief to focus on that rather than her own mysterious past. There were all the answers she needed in the back of her mind, so close, yet just out of reach. Not for the first time she had the odd sensation of apprehension and reluctance to face those memories. Rather than brooding, she chose to have this one afternoon free of questions and anxiety. She could face her ghosts later.

Just one afternoon with him, she thought. Was that so much to ask?

Tyler knew exactly where he was taking her. There was a blanket in the back of the Jeep, along with a thermos of coffee. Back in the old days when he needed to escape from the tension at home, he had headed up Lamb's Canyon to an isolated, high mountain meadow several miles east of town. He had spent hours and hours there, wondering about his future and wishing for something, *anything,* to happen to him. Of course, in those days there had been only a rutted dirt road winding up the mountain, so he'd usually saddled a horse and cut across country. It had been more than a decade, and Lamb's Canyon had caught up with the times. The Jeep followed a curling ribbon of paved road, winding up and away from the little town of Bridal Veil Falls. Then Tyler turned off the main road and left the Jeep idling while he unlocked a steel pipe fence with a sign that said No Trespassing.

"You're the sheriff," Jenny pointed out from the passenger seat. "You can't trespass."

"I have the key to the gate, silly rabbit," he said. "I know the owner. And why all of a sudden are you intent on *keeping* laws?"

"I've reformed." She couldn't help the silly, love struck smile that curved her lips. Tyler's broad-shouldered figure was outlined against a bluebird sky, his burnished hair haloed in sun. There was a frayed white hole in the knee of his stone-washed jeans, and the cowboy boots he had donned were scuffed and obviously well-worn. Jenny wondered if she had ever known a cowboy before. She rather doubted it, or she wouldn't have been riding a Harley-Davidson alone. She had discovered she was particularly susceptible to cowboys. And sheriffs.

They drove another half mile, this time on a narrow gravel road. Jenny saw two deer shaded in the aspens, a mother and her fawn. She also doubted she had seen many deer, or she wouldn't have whooped and pointed and felt as if she had witnessed a miracle right there in Lamb's Canyon. Tyler found her excitement highly amusing. Who would have guessed the sullen rebel from Enchilada Ernie's would have been capable of so much childlike enthusiasm?

The dirt road abruptly ended in a small gravel clearing. Tyler parked the Jeep, then turned to Jenny with a grin. "See?"

Jenny followed the sweeping gesture of his hand, gazing on a mountain meadow of wildflowers. She'd never seen such colors—vivid reds, butter yellows, the lavender paint-spots of bluebells. There was a tiny lake at one end of the meadow, fed by a stream that appeared magically out of the rocks in the side of a sloping hill. And if she turned her head and glanced behind them, she could see the miniature houses and streets of Bridal Veil Falls.

"I see," she whispered, frozen in her seat. So much beauty, packed into one tiny little valley. "Tyler, this is amazing. Listen…it sounds like the aspen trees are whispering, talking. And that baby waterfall coming out of the mountain—where does it come from? Are there deer around here, too? Do you think we could pick some wildflowers for Rosie? Who owns—"

"Silence, angel. What a little motormouth," Tyler observed mildly, his soft blue eyes lit with amusement. "Would you like to get out? I have something else to show you."

With Jenny limping and leaning heavily on Tyler's arm, they crossed to the middle of the meadow, knee-deep in wildflowers and rustling green grass. Jenny loved the soft brushing sounds they made as they walked, loved the rich, evergreen scent in the air and the sun warm on her head and arms. She had left her baseball cap in the Jeep, shaking her wild copper curls free. This place had a strange, fairy-tale feel to it, the sloping mountainside crowded with enormous pines, bluebells heavy on their fragile stalks, the gentle sounds of splashing water underscoring the idyllic scene. Once she tugged on Tyler's shirt and said confidingly, "I don't think in my *actual* life that I've spent much time walking through wildflowers. I feel like Dorothy in *The Wizard of Oz* walking through the poppies."

"You're much, much prettier," Tyler told her, his hands framing her face, his thumbs brushing her cheeks and encouraging her delighted smile. There was a mist of yearning in his eyes, a gentleness to the curve of his expressive mouth. He loved her like this, free of defenses and at peace with the world. Of course, he had loved her when she was a rebelette on a bike, loved her when she ate and couldn't pay for it, loved her in a baseball cap with her ponytail whipping behind. He pretty much figured he would have loved her in any situation, any mood, any circumstance. And he especially loved her when they were beautifully, joyously alone.

Mentally he formed the words for the first time. *I love her.*

There had been a time in his life when the prospect

of falling in love with someone would have scared Tyler Cook to death and beyond. Now it merely stunned him. He'd known it was happening all along, yet it still demanded a moment of truth.

Standing there in the meadow, alone with the sun and the earth, he opened his mouth to tell her. He wanted to tell her, but the words wouldn't come. There was something in her eyes, something in the relaxed set of her shoulders and her winsome smile that made him rethink the impulse. Jenny didn't even know who she was at the moment, let alone who she loved. And for all he knew, she could have a fiancé somewhere. Or a boyfriend. Or someone she was dating. Or a thousand other scenarios that made him turn away from her to hide the wealth of emotion in his eyes. He needed to be patient, he told himself. He needed to think about her right now, not about himself. Later—with any luck—the snarl would unravel, all the questions would be answered and he would have his chance. That was all he wanted, the chance to show her how he felt. The emotions were so strong, he couldn't imagine she wasn't feeling the same way.

Time. She needed time. And he needed a bullet to bite on.

He spread the quilt he'd brought along smack-dab in the middle of the meadow, the grasses and wildflowers providing a thick cushion for them to sit on. It was like being on an outdoor feather bed, and Jenny wiggled and stretched with delight.

"I don't think I've done this before, either," she told Tyler. He was sitting cross-legged next to her, looking down with a benevolent smile. "I would have remembered this. I swear, if I owned this land, I would live on a blanket just like this."

"It would get dicey," Tyler pointed out, "when the snow hit."

"Details." Her expressive eyes smiled up at him. "Right now I don't feel like worrying about details." Her voice softened. "Or anything else. So what's this place called?"

"Mine," Tyler said.

Her eyes stretched. "What, you own this? This whole meadow?"

"The whole mountain," he said almost apologetically. "I had to find places to stash my winnings and endorsement money, or Uncle Sam would have had a heyday with me. One of my investments was this mountain. It's part of what I call The Big Picture."

Jenny stared up at him, fascinated by the way the wind lifted his hair and spread it across his brown forehead. She also had a very good view of the cleft in his chin and the soft rise of powerful, well-defined chest muscles beneath his "Java-Enabled" T-shirt. She decided she liked this particular angle of Tyler Cook. "And what is The Big Picture?"

Grinning, he stretched out beside her, clasping his hands beneath his head. "Since you asked so nicely, I'll tell you. Right now you're sitting on my front porch."

Jenny looked to her right and left. "I am?"

"Yes. It's a deep, covered porch that wraps around the entire house."

"What house?"

He looked at her, blue eyes chiding. "Have some imagination, will you? The house is built with river rock and logs. It has a green metal roof to match the trees, so it blends in to the surroundings. There are two fireplaces, one in the great room and one in the bedroom.

On the front door there's a sign that says "No Twins or Mothers Of Twins."

Jenny punched him in the arm, registering the steel in his muscles. "You don't mean that. You love those little boys. And you adore your sister."

Tyler grinned. "A man needs his space. Oh, and I forgot the most important part—there are rocking chairs on the front porch. In my old age I will sit in a rocker on my front porch and simply look at the view."

"*Ohhh.*" Intrigued, Jenny got into the game. "And will you chew tobacco and spit, like you see in all the old Western movies? And whittle?"

He cocked one dark brow at her. "Please. Do I *look* like I chew tobacco? Or whittle?"

At this, Jenny's smile slipped slowly away. Tyler looked like something she would have hardly dared conjure in a dream. The hard line of his cheek was softened with sun; his summer eyes beguiled. She could see an almost imperceptible scar on his chin, another just above his collarbone. Rodeo must be the original extreme sport, she thought. Hazardous to your health. Still, he looked good with his war wounds, a man who had loved the challenge of pitting himself against the unknown. He was so different here in this setting, a bit wilder, perhaps, and definitely more relaxed. No walls, no doors, no town to watch over and protect. Freedom looked awfully good on him.

"No," she said softly. "You don't look like a man who would whittle. You do look like you belong here, though. With things that aren't...cultivated. Things you can tame."

Tyler stared at her for the longest time. His gaze touched on the hair curling on her shoulders, her star-tipped eyelashes, the depths of her dark, intense eyes.

He lifted a gentle finger, touching the bruise on her cheekbone. "I used to think I was pretty good at taming things. Until I met you. You've got me thinking twice, kiddo."

She tried to smile, but it was something of an effort. Desire, still lingering in her body, pricked at her like hot needles. She thought, how could anyone resist someone who looks like you? "Well, I wouldn't want you to get bored with me."

"No way," he said with feeling. "That's not even a possibility. Jenny, you've inspired a wealth of feelings inside me, but none of them comes close to boredom. You're like a powder keg giving off sparks, very unpredictable. Heaven knows, I can't anticipate you."

She looked away at that, staring at the flawless blue sky until her eyes watered. Her ankle was hurting a bit, her heart was in her throat and her mind was far too crowded with far too many thoughts. Some were vivid, recent memories. Others were vague and mysterious, somehow unsettling. She pushed it all away, wanting nothing more than the healing magic of this place and this moment.

"Try," she heard herself say, her voice unusually husky. "Try to anticipate me right now. Tell me what I'm feeling right now."

A heavy silence fell, the faint amusement between them evaporating. Tyler studied the perfect outline of her profile while his heart came loose, skipping from his toes to his throat and back again. There was a sensuality in her voice that was unmistakable. A curiosity. And, unless he was very mistaken, a silent reply to an unspoken question. He hadn't expected such surprising candor. But when had she done anything that he'd expected?

"What do you want to feel?" Tyler asked quietly. Too quietly.

At that, she turned her head, letting him see the haunted expression in her dark eyes. Oddly, it seemed utterly natural to be here with him, though the faint brush of his thigh against hers constantly reminded her of the siren's appeal of the erotic land beyond friendship. "Don't you know by now? I want it all. I want to feel *everything*."

"I can give you that," Tyler said.

It was his last cool, logical thought. Excitement coiled deep and hard in his stomach as he rolled on top of her in a fluid motion and slanted his lips against hers. Jenny gasped, feeling every hard, aroused inch of his body on hers. Her eyes closed weakly as his hands splayed over the bare skin of her midriff, stopping just below the burgeoning curve of her breasts. He murmured something over and over—her name—but she couldn't concentrate. She was lost in this new path they had taken together. Sanity became a restless, reckless blur as they kissed in wild, hungry ways. Backlit with sun, she saw Tyler's face quickly transform with passion, his eyes heavy-lidded and hot, focused with burning intensity on *her*. They kissed as if it were the first time, the last time, the best time. And all on a pillow of wildflowers.

One of his hands clasped hers, fingers threading together in a white-knuckled grip. The other hand pushed her sweater higher, cupping the heavy, aching weight of her breast. No bra. Just sweet, sweet skin and the ultra softness of cashmere. With satisfaction he heard the sound she made, felt her back arch as she instinctively pressed against him, into him. Fiery urgency ran like rain in his body. He allowed his lips to replace his kneading fingers, touching her with liquid fire. She took a hard breath, tangling her hands in his hair. The sensations he aroused were so vivid, so powerful, she felt tears behind her closed eyelids. Everything, she thought. I want it, I want it....

Still kissing her with glutted hunger, he rolled onto his back in a fluid motion, spreading her over him. Little by little they sank deeper into their bed and their fantasy. At first it was enough, holding, kissing and touching. Even the frustration they created was exquisite, a tantalizing, building suspense. And then, without warning, the holding and kissing was spent and they needed something else to fill the void.

Jenny's hips writhed as she tumbled against him like a playful kitten, heat building. His hands stroked down her back, her buttocks, massaging and pressing her harder against him. It didn't matter that they were far away from the privacy of a bedroom. Jenny allowed her mind to drift into an unguarded state of quiet intimacy and tantalizing possibilities. Nature's backdrop was perfect for this most elemental and beautiful act. For the first time, she acknowledged to herself what he was to her, a direction she needed to follow, an inexplicable feeling of being reunited with someone or something that had deserted her long ago.

Her eyes darkened as she looked down at him through the silky curtain of her hair. "I didn't know it would be like this," she said hoarsely, her mouth honeyed and swollen. "So good..."

"You should have *asked* me," Tyler muttered, losing pace with his heartbeat. His body shifted again, sliding her beneath him. His chest made a questing pressure against her breasts. The contact sent pleasure shocks through her veins, and an aching need was born deep within. She hadn't known she was capable of so much feeling, every nerve in her body tingling and shuddering to life. His hips captured hers with gentle strength. His tongue strokes instinctively carried an imitation of the physical act they shared.

Jenny startled herself by taking his hands and placing them on her, *there,* where she ached. "Touch me, please…"

The last vestige of his control died with her pleading whisper. He buried his face in her cool hair with a groan, feeling her back arch as his hands began to work magic. She whimpered, groaned, slipped her shaky hands into the pockets of his jeans and tugged fiercely. She knew she wanted and needed more of this magic he had. There was no shame, just desire. Her fingers fumbled at his shirt, wanting to feel skin. Anticipating her needs, he rose up and tugged his shirt over his head, tossing it into a carpet of grass and flowers. Then gently he lifted her, so they were kneeling, facing each other. Holding her eyes with his, he took the hem of her sweater and pulled it over her head. Jenny closed her eyes briefly, feeling the soft, flower-scented air caressing her naked skin. Her mouth dropped open in a soft, round O. A feeling of wantonness rolled through her in a hard wave. She *liked* being like this. She was a wanton. How lovely.

Then she opened her eyes, showing Tyler the force of her emotions. They came together hard, chest to chest, in a deep, almost shocking explosion of feeling. Hands, tongues, legs, hips…they lost pace with their breathing in a blizzard of hard kisses. Jenny became frantic for some kind of release. This dark river of passion was amazing, but it seemed there was never, never enough. She couldn't have stopped now if her life depended on it. She couldn't think beyond her own need.

Clothes were stripped off impatiently, one helping the

other. They went down together on the quilt, Tyler's lips slanting a bruising pressure on hers. Skin to skin, body to body, hard bone and pliant muscle. They couldn't get close enough. Jenny's skin felt hot, flushed, colored with deep red roses and pale pink ribbons. She felt pink all over, a melting, red-hot pink....

Tyler's mouth dipped to hers again and again, then slowly moved downward, finding the turgid points of her breasts, teasing her, suckling her into a delirium of pleasure-pain. Jenny was incoherent, trying to tell him what she needed, but unable to form words. Then she realized he knew exactly what she needed. His fingers were as adept as his lips, slipping below Jenny's waist, spreading hot honey and fiery sparks. He was far more in control, managing to talk to her in hoarse gasps while he tortured her so beautifully.

"Sweetheart...I've waited so long. All my life...you feel so good...do you like this? Tell me...oh, baby, I can't wait anymore..." And cautiously, cradling her face between his palms, he sank by sweet, slow inches within her.

Jenny's eyes were wide-open, but she could hardly see anything but a sun-bright sky. Never before had life flowed through her with such incredible, perfect pleasure. She was invaded, filled, utterly complete. That sensation alone nearly brought her to rapture. Tyler lifted his head, his eyes glittering like diamonds. She saw the hard movement in his throat as his fingers brushed her hair away from her face over and over. He was biting his lip, as if trying to find some measure of control. His eyes made a slow scan of her face, from her stubborn chin to the upsweep of her brow to the ruffled tangle of her hair spread like a fan over the quilt. Memorizing, Jenny thought. Roses in winter...

Jenny's own throat was painfully tight; her heart was jumping hard in her chest. She could hardly believe the way he looked at her, as if she were a miracle. And then she lost pace with her thoughts, because something fierce and wonderful was happening deep in her belly. Radiant waves of heat were shivering downward, as if someone had turned a stove on simmer in the core of her body. Her breasts were aching badly, her stomach muscles knotted with a strange, ever-growing tension. She closed her eyes, giving herself completely to the deep, drum-primitive rhythm of her blood.

"You're so beautiful," Tyler whispered, "it breaks my heart just to look at you."

She touched his lips with a hot, shaky hand. And then, as if planned, their bodies began to move together in an age-old dance. It was the most amazing thing—Jenny could actually *feel* all the colors of the wildflowers, bright and dark, red and yellow, like a sunset coming to life inside her. But there was more...so much more. Gradually Tyler quickened his pace, taking her from astonishment to recklessness to frenzy. With every hard stroke, Jenny needed more, and then she thought if the feelings were any stronger, she would die. Trapped in her own needs, she was mindless, aching, shivering. Trying to find something familiar, she focused on his blue, blue eyes. His cheeks were hotly flushed, like a boy who had been too long in the sun. His hair was tangled in his eyes, wild and dark. He looked so young. But there was nothing young or innocent about the way he moved, about the feelings he aroused in her.

Jenny felt her spirit slipping away, her body catching fire against his. No longer was she cautious or defensive. She didn't even know who that cautious, defensive girl was at this point, nor did she care. She was yielding and completely feminine, humming with nature's most powerful energy. Her hands clung to his shoulders, her belly strained against his, every fiber of her being reaching out to him. Only him.

"Please," she whispered, drowning in dark excitement. "Help me…"

"I will." The hard brown muscles of his chest rippled with strain as he took her higher, past control. Jenny's eyes widened, the force of her sensations stunning her. She was desperate, her body literally aching with the need only he could soothe. Her eyes started to mist with pleasure tears, and Tyler's control snapped.

With a hoarse cry, he arched into her, driving harder and farther into her center. Jenny was writhing, throwing her head back, biting down on her lip hard enough to spring a drop of blood. He heard her hoarse cry of amazement. And the knowledge that he had done that for her took him over the edge of oblivion. He was one with her, sharing every movement, every pulse, every shuddering breath. Male and female, light and dark, heaven and hell…it was all combined together in one blinding, dizzying moment of delicious, addictive pleasure. The sun, the sky, the trees that whispered and the fragile wildflowers nodding in the breeze—it was all a part of them. It was so much more than sensual pleasure and release. It was an act of forgiveness, promise and sheer, sweet beauty.

It was an act of love.

Eight

The sun was bleeding on the horizon when the Jeep finally turned into Tyler's driveway. It had been a silent ride home, but not lonely. Tyler talked to Jenny with his eyes, paying equal attention to her and the road. He kept one hand on the steering wheel and one on her thigh, just touching her, as if he was afraid she would disappear. His blue eyes were heavy-lidded and slightly glazed. He was spent, still amazed at the animal burn that had taken him and Jenny over the edge into oblivion. He also discovered that true desire had no rest. Each time he looked at her Hershey-bar eyes and swollen lips, he felt the fierce need stirring again. And though she said nothing, a permanent smile lingered in her gaze. She looked soft and unfocused, like someone having a particularly sensual dream.

That dream went on, undisturbed, until Tyler realized he had company. Paradise had unwelcome visitors.

There was a Geo in his driveway, along with Rosie's station wagon stuffed with car seats. A little Geo, for crying out loud. It wasn't Grady; he owned a big, bad truck. In fact, all of Tyler's manly friends owned big, manly cars. He didn't know a soul in the world who owned a Geo.

"Friend of yours?" Jenny asked, trying not to sound disappointed. She had had hopes that Rosie would be gone and they would have the house to themselves. Very selfish, beautifully erotic hopes.

"I am a cowboy and a sheriff," Tyler said darkly. "My friends do not drive tiny cars. Most of them couldn't get inside a tiny car. Maybe Rosie has a friend over."

"Maybe," Jenny echoed, unable to disguise the disappointment in her voice.

Tyler simply couldn't let her be disappointed. He got out of the Jeep, walked around to the passenger side and opened the door. Then, without a word, he gave Jenny a hard, soul-wrenching kiss that shook her to the core. They were both gasping when he broke from her lips with a soft sucking sound. "I could ask whoever is in that house to leave," he said hoarsely, "or we could pretend they're invisible and go straight upstairs to the bedroom."

"Option two," Jenny said. Then, because Tyler looked as if he was taking her seriously, "Not really. That would be rude. Behave yourself, okay?"

"I don't want to behave myself."

"Then behave yourself temporarily."

He grinned, saluting her. "Yes, ma'am. Anything you say, ma'am. See how easy I am to handle when I'm treated properly?"

Jenny smiled lazily through a screen of lashes. "If

you'd told me from the beginning how to handle you, we wouldn't have had *nearly* as much trouble."

"You can handle me," Tyler said with feeling, "Anytime."

The living room was empty, but it sounded like the circus had set up a tent in the kitchen. Tyler could hear Rosie talking, the twins arguing...and a soft-spoken male voice he had never heard before.

A jarring thought came to mind. That attorney, Dearbourne. The missing puzzle piece to Jenny's identity. Surely the man hadn't had time to get from California to Montana. Assisting his limping love, Tyler walked slowly into the kitchen. There was a new knot in the pit of his belly and it wasn't desire related. As near as he could tell, it was fear related.

The twins had the pots and pans scattered over the floor, drumming on them with spoons. Rosie was seated at the kitchen table, opposite a fellow that Tyler had never seen before. He looked to be somewhere in the neighborhood of forty years old. He was rather slight, with neatly trimmed blond hair and a three-piece suit that screamed money. Additionally, he wore a bow tie. Tyler had thought bow ties were extinct.

The stranger looked at Jenny, his hazel eyes lighting up. He stood with gentle grace, pushing his chair away from the table. "Jenny. Oh, Jenny, I came as soon as I was contacted. Are you all right? Dear girl, you look awful. The bruises..."

Tyler didn't like the guy calling Jenny "dear." He turned to Jenny, a frown digging into his brow. She was pale, her dark eyes eating up her small face. No, not pale...she was pale *white*. Tyler had never seen that color on any person who actually breathed. Her hand was in his and he could feel it shaking badly. "Jenny?" he asked quietly. "Are you all right?"

"Eliot Dearbourne," she whispered dully. "Eliot. Of course. I know now."

"Know what?" Tyler asked, baffled. "Jenny, sit down. You look like you're going to pass out."

Still staring at Dearbourne, she seemed oblivious to Tyler's voice. "How did you find me?" she asked. "How on earth—"

"I called him," Tyler said.

Stress seemed to spin through the room. As if moving in slow motion, she turned her head and looked at him. The pain in her eyes said volumes. She didn't seem grateful. "Did you? When?"

"This morning. After that headache hit, I felt so damn helpless—I needed to find out everything I could, Jenny. I called the numbers on the business card I found in your duffel bag. It was the only way I could figure out how to help you…"

"How are you?" Dearbourne asked her. "Rosie told me what you've been through. The accident, and then your memory—"

"My memory," she replied without inflection, "is fine. Everything came back when I saw you, Eliot. Every piece of the puzzle. I'm…just…fine."

But the way she said it, Tyler knew she was anything but fine. She looked as though she hated whatever it was she had remembered. She pulled her fingers from his, pushing both hands in the pockets of her jeans. "Tell me," Tyler said. "Jenny, what's happening in you?"

She looked at Tyler, but his image had softened to a glassy blur. Reality bites, she thought through a haze of emotion. "The doctor was right. I just needed some time to heal."

Dearbourne's gaze was compassionate, infinitely kind. "Jenny, why didn't you call me before you left L.A.? You never even mentioned you were planning on going out of town. Honey, have you any idea how worried I've been? No phone calls, no messages—"

"She had a *concussion*." Regardless of how pure his motives, Tyler didn't like the bow tie calling her "honey," either. "Among other things. It's probably not the best time to put any more pressure on her."

"Of course. You're right." The blond man came a bit closer, as if to get a better view of her concussion. "The important thing is that you're all right. Are you all right?"

"Of course I am." There wasn't a shred of expression in her voice. No affection, no relief, no panic or pleasure. Her face was a blank canvas, her vivid copper curls a stark contrast to her lifeless skin. "I saw you, and…I know everything. It was all coming back to me, anyway."

"Why didn't you say something?" Tyler asked. In the back of his mind there was a painful, digging thought: did she make love with him because she knew her time with him was running out?

Jenny shrugged, wrapping her arms tightly around her chest. It was a posture he had seen before the accident, Tyler thought. Closed. "There was nothing concrete to tell you," she said. "I just knew it was imminent. Probably I would have remembered before now if—"

"If what?" Tyler prompted, touching her arm. Immediately he felt her muscles harden. This was the woman he had met at Enchilada Ernie's, distant, defensive and troubled. He felt as if a huge weight had settled on him, a far cry from the happiness he had felt five minutes earlier. "Jenny, if what?"

She smiled faintly, but there was a loneliness so vast, so bewildered in her dark pansy eyes that he could barely comprehend it. "If I'd wanted to," she said. Then, turning to her attorney, "I'm sorry you had to come all this way, Eliot. I was planning on calling you before... everything happened."

Eliot Dearbourne exchanged a look with Jenny that left Tyler standing out in a winter chill. "You know I'm always here for you. When I got the message about the accident, I didn't know whether to be relieved or panic. All I knew was that you cashed a check and disappeared. I have to tell you, my imagination has been working overtime. You sure you're all right?"

"Of course. That money you gave me last month...I bought a Harley."

Dearbourne looked horrified, as if he might hyperventilate any moment. "A Harley? As in a *motorcycle* Harley?"

"Well, it wasn't the bicycle Harley." Her voice was strained, like a violin string pulled far too tight. "If you all don't mind, I'll go upstairs and change my clothes. I didn't realize how grass stained my jeans were."

"You also have grass in your hair," Rosie pointed out. She stood up, looking with exasperation from Dearbourne to Tyler to Jenny. "Am I missing something here? Everybody seems to know all kinds of things that I don't. Jenny, where did you and Tyler disappear to all afternoon? And why do you have an attorney flying around the country on your tracks? One who gives you lots of *money,* no less. And why do you have grass in your hair?"

"Why, indeed?" Dearbourne echoed thoughtfully, catching and holding Tyler's gaze.

"Oh, put a sock in it," Tyler snapped, speaking to

both Dearbourne and his sister. He was in no mood to be polite. The woman he had made love to that afternoon bore very little resemblance to the woman he had brought home. He felt as if he'd taken one step forward and twelve steps backward. "Rosie, entertain Eliot here while I help Jenny upstairs. I'll be right back."

Rosie's cornflower-blue eyes spoke volumes to her brother. "I have *been* entertaining Eliot for three hours. He didn't come here to see *me*."

"Don't argue. Entertain him for three hours and five minutes." Tyler swung Jenny up in his arms to the sounds of her protests. "I know you can walk," he muttered. "I just feel like carrying someone, okay?"

When Tyler returned, the bow tie was sitting on a kitchen chair while Rosie was shining his shoes under the table. At least, that's what it looked like to Tyler. "What the hell is going on here?" he snapped.

Rosie looked up through a wispy screen of pale-blond hair. "*You* put a sock in it," she said. "One of the boys crawled under the table with a pink marking pen and colored Eliot's loafers. Unfortunately, I think it's sort of…permanent." She stood up, her cheeks hotly flushed. "I'm so sorry, Eliot. This kind of thing…you're probably not used to it. Unless you have children…?"

"I've never been married," he said. "And please don't worry about the shoes."

"They look really expensive," Rosie pointed out sadly.

Graciously, Dearbourne let that one pass, turning his attention to Tyler. "Is Jenny all right? I really need to speak to her."

"She's tired," Tyler said shortly. "She said she wants

a few minutes alone. Rosie, for Pete's sake get out from under the table. Where are the boys?''

"Well, they're right—'' Rosie stood up, looking around the kitchen. "Oh, wonderful. They snuck out. Excuse me please, Eliot. I have a code red.''

Eliot Dearbourne's keen green eyes followed Rosie's flight from the kitchen. "Must be quite a job,'' he commented. "Looking after those two. She probably looks forward to her husband coming home every night to help out. Do they all live here with you? Your sister and her husband and…everyone?''

Tyler plopped himself down at the table, knuckling his weary eyes with his fists. He was suddenly, strangely exhausted, as if he hadn't slept for days. "Are you asking me if Rosie is married?''

A faint smile curled the attorney's lips. Tyler had the impression this was the closest the man got to outright belly-shaking laughter. "Actually…I believe I am. I have a great many other questions for you, as well, but that's one of them.''

Tyler stared at him, unable to believe his ears. "*You* want to know if *Rosie* is married?''

Dearbourne nodded. "Yes.''

Round and round the world goes, Tyler thought in amazement, and where it stops nobody knows. "No. Rosie has never been married. She has a house of her own, where she keeps the angelic children who colored on your leather loafers. Can we talk about Jenny now?''

"Certainly,'' Dearbourne replied. He took a moment to brush a bit of lint off his lapel. "That's why I'm here, after all.''

"She didn't seem too happy to see you.'' Tyler swallowed hard. "Are you two involved?''

"As in romantically? No.''

"So you're her attorney?"

"Yes. Among other things."

Tyler was losing patience. "Well, *what* other things?"

Dearbourne looked him straight in the eye. "That's privileged information between myself and my client."

"Are you *kidding* me?" Tyler said through his teeth. "You know, if you knew me better, you wouldn't want to tick me off. A few days ago, your *client* came roaring into town trying to control a monster Harley-Davidson. Alone. Then she...misplaced...her wallet and ate a meal in a restaurant she couldn't pay for. I ended up arresting her just to keep her in one piece. That was just her first couple of hours in town. Not long after that she managed to get hit by a Pontiac trying to cross main street. I watched the whole damn thing happen and I couldn't do a thing to prevent it. And to make matters worse, the concussion she had affected her memory. I'm the one who has been taking care of her, Dearbourne. She couldn't tell me a thing about her life, but you sure as hell can."

"Why didn't you ask her upstairs?" Dearbourne said quietly. "Obviously she remembers...everything she forgot."

"I *did* ask her upstairs," Tyler told him grimly. He wondered if he would have to arrest himself if he hit this closemouthed attorney in the nose. "She said she didn't want to talk right now. That leaves me and you."

A lengthy pause. "You seem awfully concerned for a simple Good Samaritan."

Tyler looked as though it was difficult to remain calm enough to speak. "I am not 'good,' I am not 'simple,' but I'm definitely concerned. Why the hell was she out in the middle of nowhere on a stupid motorcycle that was trying to kill her?"

Eliot reached into his breast pocket for a stick of gum. Chewing gum always helped him navigate tricky situations. He chewed a great deal of gum in court. He unwrapped it, popped it into his mouth and chewed for thirty seconds before speaking. "Jenny likes to travel," he said finally. "All the time. Anywhere. Usually she'll tell me in advance where she's going, but not this time."

"And she goes alone?"

Something new came into the attorney's eyes, something anxious and wistful. "Oh, yes. Always alone."

"So what's your role in all this? You loaned her the money for the motorcycle?"

Dearbourne stood up, wandering over to the kitchen window. He took his time before phrasing his answer. "No. Jenny has no need of loans. She's extremely well-off. I simply dispersed some funds from one of her accounts at her request. I had no idea what she was going to do with it. We're friends, but I also work for her, handling her finances, investments, taxes and so on. She prefers not to do that sort of thing herself."

"What about her family?" Tyler asked. "Why aren't they involved?"

Silence. Then, "Jenny will tell you about her family when and if she wants to, which obviously she doesn't right now. It's not my place." He turned, staring long and hard at Tyler. "Now let me ask you something, if you don't mind. Actually, even if you *do* mind. If you're not a Good Samaritan, what exactly are you to her?"

A long pause followed. For whatever reason, Tyler was in no mood to be anything but blunt. "I don't know what I am to her. I only know what she is to me."

Dearbourne lifted his brows. "And that is…?"

"She's everything," Tyler said. "Everything."

"I see." Dearbourne mused silently on this, long

enough for Tyler to clench his fists. He wanted answers and he wanted them quick, but the irritating attorney seemed to be on his own timetable, staring hard at Tyler and snapping his gum repeatedly. It was a strange habit for an immaculately dressed fellow who looked and acted as if he was going to a luncheon at Buckingham Palace.

"Before Jenny realized I was here," Dearbourne said finally, "I had a good look at her. Minus the bandages and bruises, I've never seen her look happier—and I've known her for a long time. Something tells me I owe that happiness to you."

"Then what happened?" Tyler asked, shoving his chair back and starting to pace the room. He couldn't sit still while he had the sensation that his world was about to crumble. "What happened when she saw you? She was happy before you showed up, relaxed. Why did she suddenly turn into that guarded, bewildered little soul I met a few days ago? I want nothing more than her happiness, but I can't fight a nameless ghost. Somehow I have to know what's going on. Do you understand? I need some help here, all right? If you care about Jenny, give me *something*. Anything."

Dearbourne's poise never faltered, nor did his gaze waver from Tyler's. *Snap, snap.* "You're asking me to violate a client's trust."

"No, I'm asking you to tell me about your friend who I happen to care about a great deal." Tyler let out a frustrated breath. "Look, I'll make this easier on you. You don't have to offer anything. I'll just assume out loud for a minute. Jenny lives alone."

"Warm."

"And has little contact with her family."

"Cold."

"Jenny has no contact with her family?"

"Warm. Sort of."

"Okay, *that's it.*" Tyler took two steps, planting his face four inches from Dearbourne's. "I'm flat out of patience. If you care about her, tell me enough to be able to help her. I don't give a damn about attorney-client privilege. In fact, if it will make you feel better, you can call this an official police investigation. But you *will* tell me...one way or another."

Surprisingly, Dearbourne grinned. Tyler wasn't used to people who smiled when he threatened an official investigation. "You seem to be serious about this."

"Heart-attack serious," Tyler acknowledged.

"You missed your calling when you didn't become a white knight," the very dedicated attorney told the very determined ex-cowboy. "Don't clench your fists—I'm far too civilized to be in a common brawl. Also, you're bigger than me." Then, the amusement fading from his voice, "All right, sit down. There's no quick or easy way to tell this story."

Jenny couldn't come up with a reason to leave the bedroom.

Downstairs waited her past and her present. Neither of them knew much about the other. The future was nipping at her heels, spooky and dark. Her too-short time of blissful ignorance was over and gone. And there wasn't much chance of her developing another blessed case of amnesia. Damn.

Deliberately she let her mind drift back to that magical afternoon, to the revelation of life and love she'd discovered beneath a summer-blue sky. She was *glad* she'd had that, she told herself fiercely. It would give her something to cling to through the long, lonely days and months and years ahead. Granted, it was a serious deviation from her usual hands-off attitude, but she had no regrets.

Except perhaps the leaving part. That would be harder now. Tyler wasn't long in coming upstairs. She knew he wouldn't be. They'd spent such a short time together, but she felt she could anticipate him. Especially now.

The door was open. She'd been in such a state when she'd come upstairs she hadn't thought about closing it. Why should she? Everything scary was already in the room, in her mind and memories.

Still, when he walked in, tension curdled in her stomach. He knew. One look into his beautiful, somber eyes and the truth was evident. Clearly, the laughing, charming cowboy who'd made love to her that afternoon had been briefed on the lonely red-haired gypsy. Instead of love and passion, she saw sympathy.

"I should shoot Eliot," she said. "I would have preferred to have been the one who told you. Eliot's too dramatic."

Tyler sat beside her on the edge of the bed. Like Jenny, he let his hands dangle in his lap and his gaze fix on the open window on the opposite wall. In the hazy, powdery sunlight, the room took on the quality of a dream. "Is he? Then tell me. In your words. I want to hear it from you, anyway."

"Why?"

"I want to know what you feel, everything you feel."

She hadn't expected that. She closed her eyes for a moment, trying to center herself, trying to prepare. It was twice as hard now to push him away, but she had years of experience to fall back on. "Well, you know now I had a twin. We were identical. Her name was Becca. Rebecca, actually, but I always called her Becca. It was just the four of us, mom and dad and Becca and me. It was perfect, like one of those old television series where everybody says and does the right thing. It really was. The strangest things have stayed with me about that time in my life. Not the big, important things, either. Becca practicing the flute. My dad squirting us with the hose when he washed the car. And every night when we went to bed, my mom would tell us stories that starred Becca and me, and they were always cliffhangers, so we couldn't wait to go to bed the next night and see what we were going to do next. Do you know what I mean?''

Tyler's throat hurt from the force of his emotions. ''I know,'' he managed, trying to keep the sadness out of his voice. She wouldn't appreciate that. In another situation he might have envied her picture-perfect childhood, a far cry from the friction and hostility of his own childhood. But not now, not when he knew how brutally it had all ended for her. ''Eliot said your father was a builder, a contractor?''

A whisper of a smile curved her lips. ''He called it 'putting bumps on the horizon.' Sometimes on Sunday we'd all go for a ride and he'd point out all the houses he'd built over the years. He said it was his heritage, that when I was a mother and had kids of my own, I could drive past those beautiful houses and say, 'Your grandpa built that.''' Then, once again she took him by surprise. She turned her head, meeting his gaze squarely. She spoke quickly, as if afraid she might falter or, worse still, crumble right there before his eyes. ''When I was twelve years old, mom and dad and Becca were killed in a plane crash. They were going to Washington so she could play her flute in a nationwide competition. I had chicken pox, so I couldn't go.''

Tyler shook his head, a muscle working in his jaw. "That's too much," he whispered. "Too much loss."

She didn't appear to have heard him. "You know what I regret? I was so *angry* at them for leaving me. Anger and tears, that's how I said goodbye."

"You didn't know."

Jenny shrugged. "It doesn't matter now. I didn't have any family left to speak of. Eliot was a family friend and he'd been named as guardian. The poor guy has been tearing his hair out over me ever since. Not only does he have to keep track of me, but also of my money. I had a huge settlement from the airline." She forced a brittle smile. "Does that match his version? Probably not. Eliot has a hard time separating his emotions from his work. He tried to be a trial lawyer, but his genuine goodness kept getting in the way. You know, I keep getting the feeling I should have arranged weeping violins for this story."

"Stop it," Tyler said flatly.

She raised her eyebrows. "Stop what?"

"You're acting like all this is *casual*. Easy. You don't have to pretend for me. You can say what you feel."

"I *am* saying what I feel," Jenny told him. "It's been a long time, more than ten years. Believe me, I've had time to get adjusted. We're all crucified in one way or another, Tyler. None of us gets through life unscathed. I found ways to cope. Maybe I have some trouble connecting to other people, putting down roots, but that's just the way I am now. That's how I got through it all, that's how I keep getting through it all. I just keep moving on. Heart and soul, I just keep moving. Was your childhood perfect?"

"No." But it wasn't impossible. Hers had been impossible. And the only thing he could think of to say was, "I care about you, Jenny. I care so much…"

She flinched as if he had struck her. "You've only known me a few days."

Softly he said, "Sweetheart, all I needed was a few minutes."

Damn, she was starting to cry. "Don't. I'm not going to complicate things. I can't…I *can't*, Tyler."

"I'd never hurt you, Jenny."

Her eyes flashed with tearful intensity. "You can't promise me that. No one can. When we care about someone, we run the risk of losing them and being hurt. I can't lose anything more, Tyler. I can't hurt anymore. I wouldn't survive it."

"You still have a future, Jenny." Tyler forced the words through his desert-dry throat. "Your family would want you to find happiness—"

"Maybe I don't *want* happiness! How could I? They're gone, Tyler. Do you want me to just forget that? They deserve more than that. No one can take their place. Not you, not anyone."

"I'm sorry, Jenny." It was his cue, Tyler thought dully, to be sensitive. Instinctively he knew she wouldn't welcome his touch right now, so he decided to give her the only thing he could. His absence. He forced himself to stand, moving to the door in thick slow motion. "Eliot's checking into the Cotton Tree tonight. He said he had jet lag. He'll be over to see you first thing in the morning. Right now you ought to get some rest. I'll check on you later. And, Jenny?"

"What?"

He looked at her over his shoulder. She fell into his eyes, those crystal-blue eyes that hinted at strength and humor and so much life. "I want to be a part of your life," he said. "I'm not going to give up. You're going to have to find a way to cope with that."

Before she could respond, Tyler closed the door between them.

Nine

The house settled into a strange, rather fragile quiet. Obviously Rosie had taken the boys home, or the walls would still have been shaking. Apparently Eliot had gone to the infamous Cotton Tree, and Jenny hadn't seen hide nor hair of Tyler since he'd brought her dinner— chicken noodle soup and toast. "Not homemade," he told her, "but just pretend. Chicken soup is good for the soul." He gave her a brief, sexless kiss on her brow. "Sweet dreams, Jenny."

And that had been that.

The old restless spirits had taken hold of Jenny again. She limped around the room, sat at the window seat, got into bed then limped around the room again. She was tired in so many ways. Her body felt achingly weary, still warm, soft and sensitive from Tyler's lovemaking. Her mind was taut, fragile, buzzing, weary. Still she couldn't sleep.

She picked up the dog-eared copy of *American Cowboy,* reading the article about Tyler three times. One paragraph in particular caught her fancy:

> More than one jaw has hit the ground in amazement at this man's incredible talent. His work ethic is uncompromising—he's eaten more dirt than anyone else and then some. Be it saddle bronc, bareback or bull riding, Cook shows more determination to win than cowboys who have devoted their entire careers to just one of the rough stock events. This guy has shown the rodeo world that he means business.

I'm in big trouble, Jenny thought.

The last time Tyler had looked at the digital clock on his bedside table, it read 2:00 a.m. He hadn't slept a wink yet, and didn't really plan on sleeping anytime in the immediate future. There was too much going on in his mind, too many conflicting emotions. He continually restrained himself from going to Jenny's room and checking on her. It wasn't so much her health he feared for any longer. It was *his* health. What would he do, how would he feel if he went across the hall and found her bed empty?

And so he lay stretched out on his bed, clad only in low-slung boxers, arms hooked behind his head. What was he feeling? Frustration that someone he loved had been stripped of all her security at such a tender age. Anger—oh, there was definitely anger, but he didn't know who inspired it or what to do with it. He also knew fear, fear that her scars ran too deep to allow him to become necessary to her. And, oddly enough, apprehension about his next move. What was in Jenny's best interest here? Clearly she wasn't prepared for a life like his. So many things had been decided about his life a long time ago. He had his job, his sister, the twins and Ella to look after. Without him, Justin and Jamie had no father figure, and Rosie had no one to fall back on. Tyler was well and truly a permanent fixture in Bridal Veil Falls whether he liked it or not. Jenny was as much a product of her childhood as he was, with the opposite results. Where he had finally become a stickler for responsibility, she had become an ardent fan of perpetual freedom. From what Dearbourne said, she had always held back from taking happiness as her due. She felt she wasn't entitled to it, as if it somehow betrayed her lost family. Any way Tyler looked at it, it would be a major undertaking for her to rearrange the entire course of her life. After discovering all she had endured, he knew why she would be reluctant to even try. *We're all crucified one way or another, Tyler. None of us gets through life unscathed.*

Still, the door they had opened that afternoon hadn't closed for him. Every emotion he had felt then, he felt now. Even his body seemed to be remembering, his skin prickling and hot as though he had stayed in the sun too long. He'd never felt so alone.

It had been five hours since he last saw her. He missed her.

Then, as if his thoughts had conjured her up, he saw her in the doorway. She was framed in shadows, covered from head to toe in Rosie's pink nightgown. Her eyes were round and unblinking, her hair loosely braided down her back. In her hands she carried the little stuffed sheep-wolf. She looked like a character from *Little Women.*

"What are you doing?" he whispered hoarsely.

She put her finger to her lips, shaking her head. "Don't ask, Tyler. I don't know what I'm doing."

He sat up, his heart kicking into double-time. Limping only slightly, she crossed the room toward him, holding the stuffed animal against her chest like a security blanket. It actually occurred to Tyler that he had fallen asleep finally and this was his reward—a wonderful dream. That was fine with him. He'd take Jenny Maria Kyle any way he could get her, dreaming or awake. "I don't know what to do, either," he said. "Jenny, I'm lost."

"That's all right. Tonight at least we'll be lost together." She looked down at her stuffed animal, then handed it to Tyler with a strange little smile. "Hold him, please. I didn't mean to bring him along…I was cuddling up with him for comfort when I decided I had to see you."

Head spinning, Tyler automatically took the toy. "Had to see me? Why?"

In one fluid motion Jenny pulled an enormous amount of pink flannel up and over her head. She wore nothing beneath but a few fading bruises. The hazy light of a full moon slanted in the room, casting an ethereal glow on her copper hair and luminous skin. If she was self-conscious, she gave absolutely no sign of it.

"I love you, too," she said. And if Tyler hadn't known better, he would have sworn there was as much sorrow as there was sensuality in her soft brown eyes.

His heart slammed into his ribs. It took him a moment to find his voice. "Then come and get lost with me."

They came together hotly, rolling like children on the bed, giving openmouthed, scattered kisses wherever their lips could reach. There was an urgency about tonight, as if they both expected the real world to come tapping them on the shoulder with the news: "Time's up. Back to your lives you go."

Skin against skin, they yearned together, legs kicking at the sheets and arms tangling around one another. His hands were everywhere, on her face, in her hair, on her breasts, lower. She pulled his head blindly downward until his mouth was on her nipple, working dark magic. She was lost in sensations, discovering that everything they'd felt that afternoon had only grown hotter, stronger, better. There was no hesitation tonight. No questions asked or answered. He kissed her eyelashes, her neck, the sides of her temples. He touched her with hands and lips wherever he could.

Jenny was mindless and shivering almost from the first moment of feeling her naked skin against his. This was what she wanted, a moment out of time to forget. One more chance to know what it felt like to be held and loved unconditionally. She gave Tyler back equal measure, feeling no shame or embarrassment as she explored his body with her mouth and fingers. Her experiences with men were limited to an ill-advised, quietly disappointing night while in college. It was curiosity more than anything, but she discovered she preferred abstinence to disappointment.

But Tyler Cook was different. He seemed to know her soul as intimately as he was coming to know her body. He knew her sensitive spots, knew what things made her wild and what things made her desperate for relief. Floating in a square of moonlight on the bed, she memorized his image above her—the bright, love-hazed eyes, the shimmer of passion on his hard muscles, silky dark hair tangled and damp. Roses in winter, she thought, memorizing.

He made short work of his boxers with an endearing

lack of grace. There was no clothing to separate them, no doubts. They both wanted this as badly as they wanted their next breath. Or perhaps even more. Tyler's body was incredibly beautiful to Jenny—the shadowed hollows that defined his muscles, the fire and steel that came beneath. Painfully vivid sensations doubled and redoubled in her body, bringing her even higher.

Tyler's fingers splayed over her breasts as he slowly positioned himself within the cradle of her hips. He saw the wild desire in her eyes and heard her gasping his name over and over. His name…hearing it on her wet, swollen lips made him feel more loved than he had ever been in his life. Then her eyes fluttered closed and she gasped as he pressed himself intimately against her. "I want you to look at me," he told her in a ragged voice. "Look at me now, Jenny."

Through a haze of desire, Jenny barely heard the words. She forced herself to focus on him, to cling to the wild blue eyes above her. She was caught there, suspended in the emotion she saw. She couldn't have looked away if her life depended on it. The nerves beneath her skin felt as if they were rapidly beginning to fray, while at the same time, the unrelenting need of her body kept urging her on, steadily climbing higher. More pain, more comfort, more tension, more pleasure…she wanted and felt it all in a cacophony of physical sensations. Her body and her mind were both entranced.

Above her, Tyler's light-filled eyes darkened to the color of the ocean after a storm. Perspiration shimmered over his hard cheekbones. Jenny was possessed by the weight and strength and scent of this man. At some point, they had ceased to be individuals. They were one, looking for the same answers, the same relief. They were moving in rhythmic unison, moaning and writhing on the bed in a seizure of intimate need. Jenny's fingers dug into his shoulders, her lifeline as she stood on the edge of an exquisite precipice. She was spiraling out of control, first toward a sky of blazing fireworks, then swirling into a maelstrom of sweet release. And through the midst of it all, she held fiercely to his eyes, knowing, for this moment at least, she wasn't alone.

Thank you, she thought. Thank you.

In his not-so-long-ago glory days, Tyler Cook had faced down half-crazed Brahma bulls, seriously disturbed mustangs and man-hungry rodeo queens with big hair and itchy ring fingers. Through it all, he'd never once experienced even the slightest case of the jitters.

Those days were over. Right now he was absolutely terrified.

The problem was, he'd woken up alone. He hadn't been aware of Jenny leaving him in the night, which troubled him even more. Had she deliberately sneaked out? Had she left the house, as well as his bed? Though she had surrendered to her need for him last night, he couldn't shake the feeling that his hold on her was fragile. Possibly because he knew in his heart it was. Even in the deep, sweet recesses of passion, he knew she was holding something back.

He found jeans and scrambled into them as he crossed the room, hopping first on one leg and then the other. From his doorway he could see the clown room. The bed was made. No Jenny.

His heart took up residence in his throat. He took the stairs two at a time, coming up short when he saw her framed in the open front door. She was dressed in low-slung jeans with a soft cotton tee that left her midriff bare. Gypsy clothes. The diamond in her belly button winked at him.

She held the morning paper in one hand and a mug of coffee in the other.

"Good morning," she said curiously, raising an eyebrow at his state of panic. "I don't think I've ever seen anyone come down a flight of stairs so quickly—unless they were falling down head over heels. Are you all right?"

"Are you?" Tyler asked stupidly. He was realizing that fear could make a man panic. Cool Hand Luke he wasn't.

"Of course I am." Jenny smiled, but it was a smile that didn't reach her eyes. She brushed past him, leaving the fragrance of apple shampoo in the air. "Come in the kitchen. I fixed us something to eat. I don't exactly cook, but I *can* butter toast."

"Jenny—"

"Come on, things are getting cold. Your sister called while you were sleeping like the dead. She wants you to call her."

Tyler followed her into the kitchen, trying to catch her hand in his and missing. His panic turned to a cold apprehension. She didn't want to be touched. That hadn't been her attitude last night. Obviously, something had changed. "Jenny, what in the devil—"

"Your toast is getting cold," she said, taking a seat at the table. It was neatly set, blue stoneware on two place mats. There was toast, jam, coffee and cream. A nice little breakfast for two. "I was going to squeeze some fresh juice, but you don't have any oranges."

"How interesting." Tyler remained rooted to the floor. Dread curled like something dead and cold in his belly. "I feel like I came into a movie halfway through. A very *complicated* movie. Did I miss something?"

"Not at all," she said lightly. "You're a cowboy and a sheriff, remember? Not the kind of guy to miss anything important. Are you going to eat your toast?"

"No, I'm not going to eat my toast! When did you get up?"

She took a bite of toast, her gold-tipped lashes swept downward, covering the expression in her eyes. "I'm not sure. Around five, I think. I'm a terrible insomniac. Have been since…forever. Can I have your toast, then? I'm starving."

Tyler shook his head helplessly. "What is *with* you?"

Still avoiding his eyes, Jenny chewed for a moment before answering. "Morning-after nerves, maybe. It's hard to know the etiquette, y'know? I'm not exactly an expert when it comes to…comes to…"

"When it comes to what?"

"What we did," Jenny finished lamely.

"What we did," Tyler told her, "is make love, physically and emotionally. Is that so hard for you to say?"

Again she avoided his eyes. "Of course not."

But you still didn't say it, Tyler thought. Although it was warm in the sunny kitchen, he felt a little chilled. Something serious was going on here, and he couldn't seem to get a handle on it. "Jenny, let's just back up a little here. The last thing I remember you saying last night is 'I love you.' The only thing you want to talk about this morning is toast. Yesterday you were one person, today you're another."

"No," Jenny said, pushing back her chair and heading for the sugar bowl on the counter. "Yesterday I was confused. Today I'm me again, warts and all. That's the only difference. Don't look so worried. I'm fine."

"I'm *not* worried about you," Tyler snapped. "I'm worried about *me* right now. I woke up alone this morning. Even now that I'm with you, I still feel alone. That's scary, particularly when I've got my heart out on a limb like this. Just tell me—"

Then came a knock on the front door. It was a very precise knock—shave-and-a-haircut, two-bits. An attorney's knock.

"We're not through," Tyler said. "I'm going to get rid of the visitor and we're going to talk. Yes?"

"Whatever," Jenny said lifelessly. She watched him walk out of the kitchen, her eyes following the beautiful curves and muscles of his bare back. His jeans rode low on his hips, emphasizing the cat-like rhythm of his walk. And he had pillow hair, she thought, smiling through a sudden mist of tears. All crumpled and tangled around his head.

I can't cry. She blinked her lashes furiously, taking her sugar bowl back to the table. She was going to be just fine as long as she kept her shiny new, unfamiliar emotions under lock and key.

Leaving Tyler in bed earlier that morning had been one of the hardest things she had ever done. She knew, as he did not, that would be the last time she lay in his bed.

She tried to find comfort in the old distractions: Where do I go next? What do I want to see? How long should I stay there?

It didn't work. There was no comfort in the thought of leaving him. Only panic, deep inside, viciously biting at her. It had rattled her all morning, making it terribly painful to make plans and say what needed to be said. There was guilt, as well, for deliberately letting him believe that last night was something other than…the last night. For the first time in years she had wanted something badly. For better or worse she'd allowed herself that small betrayal of her own isolation. She'd wanted the memories. Winter was coming, and she needed a few roses to cling to.

As she'd expected, Eliot followed Tyler back into the kitchen. He'd lost the bow tie and dressed down for his day in Bridal Veil Falls. Khaki slacks, a pin-striped shirt and glossy Italian shoes. The starch in his shirt seemed to be holding his upper body in a perfect posture. In his wardrobe and in his business, he was a very particular man.

"Good morning, Eliot," Jenny said with a plastic smile. "I see you've dressed for a holiday. No suspenders or tie. Are you roughing it?"

"Even I can relax under the right circumstances," Eliot told her. "How are you feeling?"

Jenny darted a quick glance in Tyler's direction. His face was still a thundercloud. "Just ducky. I've put coffee on if you'd like a cup?"

"No, thank you." Eliot looked down at his immaculate shoes. "I have an appointment for breakfast."

Tyler raised his eyebrows at him. "You have an appointment in Bridal Veil Falls?"

Eliot cleared his throat. "Indeed. A breakfast appointment."

"You said that." Jenny stared at her attorney with curious eyes. "Eliot, you don't *know* anyone in Bridal Veil Falls."

Eliot's lips curled faintly. "I beg to differ. I know you, Sheriff Cook and…his sister, Rosie. And her children. That's five people."

"And which of those five people are you having breakfast with?" Tyler asked him.

"The last three."

There was a moment of silence. Tyler thought it only fitting, since the man was going into the terrible-two's war zone for breakfast. He didn't have a clue what he was getting into. "I see," he said, though he didn't see at all. "And when did you make this appointment?"

Eliot began to wriggle ever so slightly in his starched shirt. "Last night. I called her, actually. But that isn't what I came here to talk about. Jenny, did you have a good night?"

Jenny choked on a healthy swallow of coffee. "What?"

"A good night," Tyler supplied smoothly. "The man wants to know if you had a good night. Actually, *I'd* like to know if you had a good night, too. Well?"

Jenny's skin burned hotly. She began dumping sugar into her coffee cup. "It was fine."

"Just *fine?*" Tyler asked innocently. "My night was better than fine. My night was—"

"Eliot didn't ask about your night," Jenny said hastily. "Did you, Eliot?"

Eliot blessed them both with a knowing smile. "I'm sure I hope he had a decent night, as well. Jenny, I do need to ask you something. Since I got here, I've realized how hard I've been working lately. Much too hard. Since you're not completely on the mend, I'm considering staying here for a day or two just to relax. Then we can talk about getting you home safe and sound. I think it would be good for both of us."

Jenny became absolutely still. This was a curve ball she hadn't expected. Eliot never did anything but work, *never*. He lived for his work. Why would he suddenly decide he needed a vacation? Especially when she'd half expected him to insist she return to Los Angeles with him?

"Have *you* had a crack on the head, Eliot?" she ventured.

"I have not!" he replied indignantly. "Even I am capable of being spontaneous now and again. This is a beautiful place. Why shouldn't I enjoy her? I mean, it. Enjoy *it.*"

"Whatever," Tyler muttered, feeling as if his world was spinning slightly out of kilter. "It's your neck. I'll tell you one thing, though. I wouldn't wear anything over there that you don't want food stains on. It's a jungle at Rosie's."

"I'll manage," Eliot said smoothly. "Jenny, I'll call you this afternoon and we'll make some plans. Yes?"

There was almost an imperceptible pause before she answered. "Of course. Enjoy your breakfast. Say hello to Rosie for me."

When Tyler returned from walking Eliot to the front door, Jenny was washing dishes at the sink. He could tell by her rigid posture that she was in no mood to continue their discussion. Not to mention the fact that the wall clock told him he was late for work.

"Jenny?" he asked quietly.

She glanced over her shoulder, still wearing her bright and unconvincing smile. "Can you believe that one? Eliot and Rosie. If you knew him like I knew him—"

"I don't want to know Eliot," Tyler snapped. "I want to know you. I want to know everything you're feeling and thinking and planning—emphasis on planning."

She went back to her work. "You sound like you're worried I'm going to rob the First National Bank of Bride Falls on Her Head."

"Promise me something."

There weren't any more dishes to be done, darn it. Jenny had no choice but to turn and face him, drying her hands on a dish towel. "Sure. What?"

"You won't leave while I'm at work."

"Okay."

No, Tyler thought. That came too fast. Tyler walked over to her, planting his palms flat on the counter on either side of her hips. "Jenny? I won't be gone more than a couple of hours. That's all I'm asking, two hours. There's too much unsaid between us. Promise me you'll wait until then to make any decisions." He kissed her once, hard and unexpected. "Promise me. Swear you'll stay until we can talk."

"I promise," she said hoarsely. "I'll be here."

Tyler stared at her for a long moment, trying to read her face. But she was far too good at controlling her emotions. He couldn't find truth or reassurance, nor could he see any evidence that she lied. He had no choice but to believe her.

He kissed her one more time, long and sweet and lingering. He took some comfort in the fact that she kissed him back, as openly and sweetly as she had kissed him the night before.

Then, because he had no choice, he went upstairs to shower and change.

Ten

Tyler hadn't realized Jenny's duffel bag was already packed, waiting for her in the closet of the clown room.

He left for work after giving Jenny a couple of DVDs to watch while he was gone. Also a book. Also several magazines. He seemed intent on making sure she didn't run out of things to do until he was home.

She hobbled upstairs and watched him leave from the bedroom window. She stood there long after the Jeep had disappeared, her palms pressed flat against the glass. Come back.

But it wouldn't make any difference if he did come back. She knew that now. She also knew she had lied when she'd looked straight into Tyler's eyes and told him she would be here when he came home. There was no way she could keep that promise, though she wished with all her heart it was possible. This was the simplest form of torture, one person being pulled in two directions. She needed to go. She wanted to stay.

She'd been taken completely by surprise when Eliot had opted to stay in town for a day or two. She had expected him to insist that she see a doctor in Los Angeles, particularly after spending a night at the less-than-luxurious Cotton Tree Motel. Eliot liked his creature comforts. But no, everyone in her life these days seemed to be throwing her for a loop. Even the usually predictable Eliot was acting as if he were possessed by a new, less uptight personality. She still couldn't quite get her mind around the concept of Rosie and the buttoned-down lawyer with a fetish for stiffly starched shirts. Was it something about Bridal Veil Falls that made people do things completely out of character? Maybe it was in the water.

So…this called for plan B. Which meant she had to come up with a plan B.

Her breath was quick and frightened as she pulled her duffel bag out of the closet, unzipping a little compartment on the inside seam. It was rather like Aladdin's lamp, her duffel bag. It produced several hundred dollar bills that she kept for emergencies. Enough to go…somewhere. She could leave Eliot a message at the motel. And as for Tyler…she could leave him a note. What she would say in the note was still rather vague. Her heart seemed to be hurting too much for her to even think. She only knew a fierce, unrelenting need to be alone, and quickly. If she spent too much time here, if she came to care too much…she would be vulnerable again. She would have someone in her life she couldn't live without. She couldn't bear that idea. She knew only too well how unexpectedly loved ones could disappear, and how deep and abiding the hurt was long after they'd gone.

She couldn't take the chance of going through that again. She wouldn't survive.

She knew Tyler would be all right. He had his family, his work. He had his someday ranch on the mountain overlooking Bridal Veil Falls. He wasn't isolated the way she was. He was a part of something bigger, something stronger than just himself, a limb of another body. She'd known what that was like once. It was the most precious thing in the world. There would always be loving and familiar faces around Tyler, people to share his hopes and dreams. And Jenny...she had been adrift for longer than she could remember. It was the only way she knew how to live. There was a sort of blind, unreasoning panic inside her—the emotional fallout from allowing Tyler to become almost...necessary. But that was then and this was now, and he had been everything he could be to her. Still, she had the feeling she would never quite readjust to life without him. He'd done some fair damage to her heart in a few short days. What could he do with another hour, another day, another week? She was terrified she would come to need him. Long before she'd met him, she'd known she had little left to lose—and nothing left to give.

Don't think about it. Don't think about what you're walking away from. Don't think, don't think...

She hoisted her backpack over one shoulder, taking one last look at the clown room. Bozo and his buddies had become oddly comforting in the last couple of days. When her eyes started to sting with tears, she closed them, but all she could see was Tyler's image in her mind. She knew she would see his face in her dreams from now until forever.

Downstairs she called a cab, then left a voice mail for Eliot at the Cotton Tree. It was short and to the point: "Feeling fine. Think I'll leave today. Too long in one place makes Jenny a dull girl. I'll call you in a couple of days. Sorry I caused you so much trouble."

Tyler's note was much harder to compose. She found a notepad in the kitchen and scribbled a few words, then crumpled it and tossed it in the trash. Another paper, another few words and another slam dunk in the trash. She repeated this process two more times until she realized she could never put her emotions into words. Finally she settled on two simple words: "I'm sorry."

It would have to do.

She felt a little sick as she watched the cab pull up in front of the house. The canary-yellow Ford was old enough to be considered an antique, no doubt the official and only cab in the small town. No air seemed to be getting into her lungs, no blood moving through her veins as she climbed into the back seat and told the driver to take her to the bus depot.

"There ain't no *depot* to speak of," the grizzled driver replied in a slow drawl. "Most folks just wait on the bench in front of the American Legion Hall."

Jenny closed her eyes against the headache that was threatening. "Fine. Take me to the American Legion Hall, then."

"You want Greyhound? 'Cause Greyhound is all there is."

"Greyhound's fine."

"You just walk across the street to the Piggly Wiggly to buy your ticket. Where are you headed?"

Jenny glanced nervously over her shoulder, watching for Tyler's car. If she talked to him one more time, her resolve might falter. Neither one of them could afford that. "I don't know where I'm going. But I *do* know I won't get there if you don't move this car."

"Lady, you need to relax. I don't break the speed limit for anybody. The law in this town takes the speed limit pretty seriously."

"I know all about the law in this town." Her voice was low, filled with an immense sadness. "Fifty bucks extra if you step on it."

"I can do that."

She bought a ticket to St. Paul, Minnesota, because it was the next bus scheduled to come through town. She was lucky with the timing—the ticket agent told her there were only two buses that went through Bridal Veil Falls each day, one headed east and one headed west. Jenny had only an hour to kill, an hour she spent wandering around in the produce section of the Piggly Wiggly, hoping against hope that she could get on the bus before Tyler came to find her.

If he came. After he'd realized that she had left, he could very well say good riddance. And she wouldn't blame him a bit.

By the time she boarded the bus, she was feeling sick with nerves. She couldn't think back to a time when a place had been so hard to leave...or a person. She told herself she would feel better when she was in a new place, with new scenery, new experiences. There were several other people already on the bus, each one wearing identical expressions of fatigue and boredom.

She missed him already. Oh, how she missed him.

She turned blindly toward the grimy window next to her seat, then realized her thoughts had conjured the man. He was heading out of the Piggly Wiggly toward the bus, obviously a man with a mission. His lips were tight, his eyes stony. His beige uniform proclaimed him as the law. Jenny began to perspire. He was in Gladiator mode.

The next thing she knew, he was standing in front of her, both hands clenched into tight fists. Jenny had never seen his muscular arms straining with so much tight energy.

"Fancy meeting you here," he snapped. "Nice note you left me. I was overwhelmed. I want you to get off this bus."

"I can't."

"Yes you can. And you will."

Panic and pain made Jenny babble. "What are you now, the bus police?"

Softly, but with a bite, he said, "This isn't the place to talk, Jenny. We can work this out, but you have to stay around long enough to find a way. You have to help me. This is one thing I can't do alone."

"You're holding up these people," she muttered, glancing toward the older woman seated across the aisle. She wasn't looking bored any longer. She looked quite entertained. "Tyler, there's nothing left to—"

"Don't." He closed his eyes briefly, wondering what expression was on his face. Fear? Anger? Confusion? He felt all three. Then he looked into Jenny's eyes and saw the dark wounds there. He felt a perverse satisfaction. At least she was hurting, too. He'd had that much of an impact on her. "I love you," he said, loud enough for everyone on the bus to listen in to their conversation. *"I love you.* What do I have to do to prove it?"

"Nothing," Jenny said hoarsely, blinking furiously against the tears that threatened. "This isn't about love."

"The hell it isn't! Do you think what we have comes along every day? Do you have any idea how long I've waited for you? And you expect me to just let you disappear?''

It took Jenny two tries before she found her shaky voice. ''I'm not disappearing. I'm going to Duluth.''

''St. Paul,'' the woman across the aisle corrected.

''I'm going to St. Paul,'' Jenny said, feeling frantic. ''I'm going because I want to. I haven't seen much of the east. It's time I did.''

''It's that easy for you?'' Tyler said, his eyes firebright with emotion. ''After…everything, it's that easy for you? 'Yes, I'll be here when you get home, Tyler. No, I think I'll go to Minnesota instead, Tyler.' ''

Jenny's eyes glittered like a startled doe's, dark and fixed. She stopped praying for the courage to do this thing well. She started praying for the courage to do it at all. This leaving was worse than she'd imagined, a thousand times worse. ''I have to go. I *want* to go. It's that simple.''

Hot blood stung his cheeks. ''Give me a reason. Give me one good reason to let you leave.''

''What are you trying to do? Force me to say things that will only hurt you? This is *your* life, Tyler. Not mine. From the very beginning, I was only passing through.''

From the front of the bus, the driver shouted something about keeping to his schedule. Tyler didn't seem to have heard him. ''It's more than that, and you know it. Jenny, I can't just walk out on my family. If I could, I swear I would, and I'd get on this damn bus and head east with you. Just give me some time to work things out.''

''I don't want you to leave your family!'' Now Jenny was well and truly frightened. Just the fact he'd even thought about leaving his family, his job, his town, cut to the depths of her. She would never ask that of him, never expect it. She knew only too well what losing a family was like. She wouldn't be responsible for that. "Tyler, we had all we could have. I'm not willing to take it any further. I don't want to. I like my life the way it is."

"I don't believe that," he said flatly.

"Well, you don't have any choice." Nothing lived in Jenny beyond the need to shelter him from the jagged remnants of her scarred life. "I was curious about you, Tyler. I satisfied that curiosity, but I never considered making our relationship permanent. Never. I care for you and I'm grateful to you, but I won't pretend to give you something I can't give. Accept it."

"You're lying."

Yes. But I'm doing it out of love. "I'm sorry, Tyler. Truly. But I don't fit here, and you sure don't fit into my plans."

"Do you know what I think?" Tyler said with deceptive softness. "You're too damn chicken to face what we could have together, Jenny. You're scared to risk your pretty neck. You'd rather run than let something *matter*."

"You've got that right." She forced herself to smile, though her stomach was spinning and jumping in a nauseating fluctuation. "I always take the path of least resistance. You should know that by now. I think the bus driver is going to have apoplexy if we don't get on the road soon."

He became completely motionless in that way he had. Still, he didn't bother to hide the stark pain in his eyes. Nor the anger. "Just like that?" he asked softly.

The crushing weight in Jenny's chest was growing heavier, harder to bear. She knew she had to end this now, before the dam broke and she flooded the Grey-hound bus with tears. "Path of least resistance," she repeated, her voice choked and hoarse, as if she had a cold. "That's me."

Tyler took one step backward, looking around the bus as if seeing the other passengers for the first time. He shook his head, trying to think beyond his ravaged emotions. Nothing came, just complete chaos.

"Goodbye," Jenny said, wanting him to leave. A monsoon was coming, compliments of her broken heart. She met his eyes, then looked away. Helplessness took her by the throat, squeezing. She wanted this to be over.

"I guess it's your call," Tyler said finally. "I'd expected more of you, Jenny. I thought you were a fighter. My mistake."

"She's the one making a mistake," someone muttered from the back seat.

It was all Jenny could do to hold her head up and her shoulders square. She felt like someone in a very bad movie that wasn't going to end well.

"Please go," she said.

Beneath his shirt, his chest was taut with strain. His neck muscles were also corded, pulsating with every beat of his heart. Effortlessly he locked her into his angry, beautiful sky-blue eyes. "You better be damn sure this is what you want, Jenny."

For one moment nothing seemed to exist in the world but the awful blankness inside her. One thing she had learned long ago—life was not about what she wanted. She forced herself to swallow over the aching knot in her throat. "Take care of yourself, Tyler."

"And since you're leaving me no choice—you better take care of yourself, as well. Apparently you'd rather have a memory than the real thing."

"Think about it," the lady across the aisle remarked. "You better think about this, honey."

Jenny couldn't think. She felt like the sky had landed with all its terrible weight on her shoulders. He had to go, he had to go now. Desperation gave her the strength to say, "The driver is going to call the police if you don't get off the bus. Then you'd have to put yourself in jail." Then, in a very different voice, *"Go."*

Tyler backed out of the bus slowly, never looking away from her once. Then he turned abruptly at the door and took the metal stairs in one step.

Outside he stood with his thumbs hooked in the pockets of his pants, his golden-brown hair ruffled in the breeze from the departing bus. And there he stood, growing smaller and smaller as Jenny got farther away.

Jenny didn't hide her tears in her hands until he was out of sight. She knew, as Tyler did not, that his memory would never be enough.

Eleven

Tyler was in a very bad mood.

It was Saturday night, his third Saturday night since Jenny had left town. Tyler had discovered he hated Saturday evenings. They were long and lonely. So lonely, in fact, that he decided to go over to Rosie's and distract himself with the terrible twins.

That was lonely, indeed.

His worry for Jenny was a barbarous, open wound, bleeding whenever he examined it too closely. She hadn't been completely well when she'd left. For the first few days he'd hung on to a faint hope that she would call, let him know where she was, tell him she'd changed her mind. After that, he'd run out of hope and all he had left was the pain.

He hadn't been exceptionally easy to be around, he knew that. He probably owed Rosie an apology. He'd been short-tempered with her, short-tempered with everyone, actually. In the back of his mind, he couldn't quite shake the feeling that his responsibilities had somehow cost him any happiness he could have had with Jenny. And though he'd accepted those responsibilities of his own free will, he was still conflicted. He'd tried for so long to fill his father's shoes, to care for Ella and Rosie and the boys the way they deserved to be cared for. Until Jenny came into his life, he'd never wondered about what *he* deserved. He'd been too busy trying to make up for all the mistakes of the past.

He'd never bothered with knocking when he visited his sister. He discovered when he swung her front door wide, however, he probably should have announced his arrival. Then he might have been spared the sight of his sister snuggled on her sofa with Eliot Dearbourne. *Kissing*.

No brother ever wanted to see his sister locked in a passionate embrace. Tyler slapped his hand over his eyes, said a bad word and shut the front door. Then he counted to ten and opened it again. Dearbourne was on his feet, slightly flushed but looking quite happy. Rosie was still sitting on the sofa with a goofy smile on her face.

"What are you doing here?" Tyler asked the attorney by way of greeting. "Why aren't you in Los Angeles? Am I going crazy, or did I just witness you making out with my sister?"

Eliot cleared his throat. "Good to see you, too. And yes, we were making out. Sorry about that." Then, on reflection, "No, I'm not."

The guy had lost the bow tie, Tyler noticed. There was nothing on his pristine white shirt but a smear of something that looked like grape jelly. Shaking his head, Tyler glared at his sister. "You want to explain this?"

Rosie thought about it. Then she said, "No. Not really."

Tyler's jaw was clenched hard enough to crack a molar. This situation was exacerbating his very bad mood. The last time he had seen Eliot Dearbourne had been the day Jenny left town. The man had called him a fool for letting her get on a bus in her condition. Tyler had come *this close* to popping him in the nose. The next day Dearbourne was on a plane to Los Angeles, never to be seen again. Or so Tyler assumed.

"Well, *someone* better talk," he said through his teeth. "Where are the boys? Where's Ella?"

"They're spending the night with my next-door neighbor," Rosie said calmly.

This had the effect of an atom bomb dropped in the living room. "You two are here alone?"

"Relax, Ty," Rosie told him, uncurling from her comfy position on the sofa. "Eliot's been a perfect gentleman. He's always a perfect gentleman. Nothing's going to happen that I don't want to happen."

"What do you mean, *always?*" Tyler demanded. "You only knew this guy for a couple of days, Rosie. You can't make a judgment on—"

"You'd better sit down," Eliot told him. "You don't look well."

"He's right, Ty," Rosie said cheerfully, patting her brother on the shoulder. "You've had a bit of a shock. Well, I for one am glad you walked in here so rudely. We were getting sick of hiding from you all the time, anyway."

Tyler sat down heavily into a leather recliner. "Hiding?"

Eliot and Rosie exchanged a look. "Eliot's been back to visit me a couple of times," Rosie said finally.

"Mostly on the weekends. The last three weekends, actually. We didn't want to tell you because...well, we were happy and you weren't, basically. I've been feeling terribly guilty."

"Oh, I can tell," Tyler said tonelessly. Under his palms on the armrests, the leather felt slippery. At least it was something to hold on to. "You're all busted up about it."

"Rosie?" Eliot asked quietly. "Would you go make us a cup of coffee or something? It might be a good idea if I talked to Tyler alone for a few minutes."

Rosie eyed her brother uneasily. "Are you going to be nice?"

Tyler groaned, dropping his forehead into his hand. "Yes, Rosie, *dear*. I'll be nice."

But the moment she was gone, he shot Eliot a warning look. "If you are taking advantage of my sister, it will be the last thing you ever—"

"You shouldn't threaten people with death," Eliot interrupted mildly. He sat down on the sofa, smoothing the creases in his slacks. "You're the law around here, after all."

"I was her brother long before I was the law." Tyler stared at Dearbourne long and hard. He was trying to make the man uncomfortable, but it didn't seem to work. The attorney maintained his calm demeanor. "What did you want to talk to me about?"

"Jenny. I was going to call you tomorrow, so you saved me the trouble." Dearbourne sighed regretfully. "Although your timing is lousy."

Jenny. The name always in his mind, but never on his lips. He hadn't talked about her since the day she'd left, despite all Rosie's efforts to make him open up. "What about her?'' he asked, his heart twisting painfully in his chest. "Is she all right?"

Eliot pursed his lips, appearing to give a great deal of thought to his response. "Well, that depends on your interpretation of *all right.* She called a couple of days ago to tell me she was doing well, and asked me to wire some money."

Tyler's head snapped up. "Wire money? Where?"

"To a bank."

Tyler's hands were now clenched into fists. "*What* bank?"

"First National in New York City. She's decided to spend the winter there. In the city, not at the bank." As a lawyer, Eliot had been trained to always clarify himself. "She actually has herself some sort of job, though she didn't say what it was. I'm feeling quite optimistic about her, to tell you the truth. She's never been interested in staying in one place for any length of time."

"That's great," Tyler said woodenly. "Just ducky. Wonderful for her."

Eliot raised a questioning brow. "Do I detect a residue of anger?"

"Why can't attorneys communicate like normal people?" Tyler snapped. "Why do you have to use words like *residue?* Yes, Eliot, I'm angry. She got on a Greyhound bus and left me flat. She wouldn't even give me a chance to make her happy. Nor has she called me, which has left me with an even bigger *residue* of anger."

Eliot walked over to the front window, staring out at the darkened street. After a long moment, he said quietly, "I'm getting to like this little town, Tyler. It's like something out of a novel, the perfect little place to live and grow. The level of simple happiness here is amazing to someone accustomed to the rush and noise and craziness of Los Angeles. That's one of the reasons I keep coming back.'' He looked over his shoulder with a little smile. ''Not the main reason, though.''

''Rosie,'' Tyler said.

''Rosie.'' The way Eliot said her name, he made it sound like an endearment. ''Do you know why it's so easy for me to fall under the spell of this place? I don't know what it's like to be completely alone in the world. I have six—count them, six—sisters. My parents are living in a retirement community in Palm Beach. We get together for holidays, birthdays, you name it. I'm one of the lucky ones who has nothing but good memories from life. I *expect* to be happy. And the prospect of committing to something—or someone—incredibly special doesn't scare me a bit.''

''Obviously, you haven't spent enough time with the terrible two,'' Tyler muttered.

Eliot smiled. ''Believe it or not, they don't scare me, either. But I realize I'm one of the lucky ones. I automatically take happiness as my due. Jenny hasn't had that luxury. She knows what it's like to lose everyone and everything. It doesn't surprise me a bit that she wouldn't stay here with you. Unlike me, she *expects* to be alone. That's been the only constant in her life for a long time—being alone.''

Tyler stood up abruptly, rubbing the back of his neck with his hand. He felt punchy with nerves, his mind exhausted. No matter how long he thought about her, he couldn't come up with a way to solve it. His conscience demanded he stay where he was. His heart didn't give a damn about his conscience. ''I tried to make her stay, Eliot. I begged her to stay. She said no.''

''Of course she said no,'' Eliot replied, shrugging. ''You asked her the wrong question.''

"Y'know, I'm really not in the mood for games. If you want to tell me something—"

"You asked her to *stay with you*," Eliot said quietly. "Of course she said no. Do you know what an enormous risk that would be to someone like Jenny? One minute she's alone and safely shut off from her emotions, the next she's in the middle of the Brady Bunch and asked to stay forever. Of course she wasn't up to dealing with that. To someone like Jenny, simple happiness is a major hurdle, an enormous risk. It's like saying to fate, 'Okay, I'll give you one more stab at me. Have at it.'"

Tyler only stared at him, a muscle working hard in his jaw. "I didn't think of it like that."

"Why would you? You two were living on an emotional roller coaster, racing from one crisis to another. I don't think you had much time to actually understand each other, or the feelings you had. When Jenny finally came back to earth, she felt she had only one choice— be absorbed into *your* life, *your* family, *your* love, or...continue as she always had, alone. Are you really surprised she bolted?"

Dearbourne was making a terrible sort of sense. "You said that I asked her the wrong question. What did you mean?"

Very deliberately he said, "You asked her to stay. You never asked her if you could go with her."

Tyler swallowed hard. "Don't you think I would have if it was possible? Rosie needs me here. The boys need me here. My job is here. This is my life, and it's way too late to change anything now."

"Why?"

"Why?" Tyler stared at Eliot. "Are you *listening?* I used up all my choices a long time ago. I spent ten years on the rodeo circuit, living from moment to moment, cheerfully risking my neck for something as stupid as money. I really didn't give a damn about what was going on here. I was the biggest disappointment in the world to my father. When he died, I realized the only way I could make up for it was to try and take his place here. To take care of the family. What makes you think I have the right to up and leave everyone who depends on me?''

"You could ask me," Rosie said. "Ask me if you have the right to up and leave me.''

Neither man had heard her come in from the kitchen. Tyler stared at his sister, feeling hot blood sting his cheeks. "Rosie. I didn't mean...I'm not sorry I came home. I love you, you know that. And the boys mean the world—''

"Give it a rest," she said, in that blunt way she had. She walked across the room to him, taking his hands in hers. "I'm just going to say this once. You're a very good man, Ty, though sometimes you have a hard time accepting that fact. I'm glad you came back, but more for your sake than mine. I know what all those years of dad's anger and criticism did to you. You needed to know you could take care of us, Ty, that you could come through for us when the chips were down. You needed to have that reassurance. And you *did* take care of us, and I'm grateful. But I'm all grown up now, and I want to make my own way. We'll always be family. Whatever we decide, wherever we go, whoever we love—'' she glanced at Eliot through a screen of lashes ''—we'll always be there for each other. It's not about the miles. It's about the love. We'll always have that. You were my hero, Ty, and I'm grateful for that. But now maybe it's time you rescued someone else.''

Tyler stared at Rosie, amazed at the wisdom of Solomon in her wide blue eyes. "What are you saying? You want me to just walk away from...everything?"

Rosie shrugged. "Not necessarily. I think of it more as walking *toward* something."

Tyler drew a deep breath, his heart lurching. He'd been dying by inches for three long weeks, achingly empty and without direction. Suddenly he recognized a new emotion within himself—something that was equal parts anticipation and disbelief. "Are you sure about this, Rosie?"

She nodded, her lips curling in a dreamy smile. "Oh, yes. Ty, you can go anywhere you want, be anything you want, do anything you want. I'll be just fine. If you want to worry about someone, you'd do better to worry about poor Eliot here."

It had been the longest month of her life.

Jenny stayed busy, with a fierce determination. Busy, busy, busy. In the daytime she volunteered at a women's shelter, providing day care for toddlers while their mothers tried to find work. At night she went to classes—classes for yoga, classes on genealogy, classes in tole painting, classes in self-defense. Every night except Saturday was filled with classes. Unfortunately, Saturdays seemed to be the day when the people who taught the classes had a life of their own. How dare they? Jenny couldn't find a Saturday class to save her life. Saturday evenings, therefore, she spent fixing up her apartment.

There was a tremendous amount of fixing to be done. Doors hung off hinges, mice cavorted brazenly, electric sockets spit and crackled at her whenever she attempted to plug anything in. Even now Jenny couldn't explain to herself why she had opted to sublet an apartment. She could have stayed in a nice hotel, could have rented a car and wandered down the coast, could have done anything and gone anywhere she pleased. Sadly, none of these options really seemed to please her. Something had happened to her in Bride Falls on Her Head. A little seed of comfort had been planted, despite all her efforts to remain untouched by her experience. She had known what it was to belong to something and someone, though only temporarily. It was addictive, that feeling of belonging.

And so, for the first time in years, she found herself trying to make some sort of home.

She wasn't experienced at nesting, that was certain. Little things like buying towels and picking out dishes were Herculean efforts. How did people match everything? How on earth did they decide what sort of bedspread they wouldn't be sick of within a month? How did they choose the color for the bedroom or pick out something major like a sofa? She changed her mind more times about more things than she could count, but still she persevered. For whatever reason, she desperately wanted something she could call her own.

She bought a coffee table, for no other reason than to display a single magazine—a worn copy of *American Cowboy*. Yes, she had stolen it from Tyler's home, stuffing it in her duffel bag before she left. Though being a thief was not a good thing, she wasn't sorry. She picked it up and looked at his face a thousand times—''Rodeo's Tyler Cook...Next Best Thing to Superman.''

How could a girl forget Superman?

Regardless of how busy she kept herself, inside she was hollow and hurting, like a wounded animal. Being alone pre-Tyler was one thing. Being alone post-Tyler was something else. She had enjoyed the incredible pleasure of waking up next to another person, a man with soul-stabbing sky-blue eyes and a smile that could bake cookies from fifty feet away. She knew what he looked like when he laughed, when he was frustrated, when he was riding a Harley and when he was terrorizing a hospital. Her mind continually gave her pictures, like a slide show of a brief, fast-burning love affair. Roses in winter. Despite the time slowly grinding by, those pictures still had enough clarity to break her heart. And the one picture that haunted her most was the vision of Tyler watching her leave town on a stupid Greyhound bus. He would never know how badly she'd wanted to scramble out the window and run to him.

But she couldn't. It was a poor reflection on her courage, but she simply couldn't make the commitment. It was too huge, too immense to contemplate. She didn't belong there. She felt like she didn't belong anywhere.

Still…she felt a part of her reaching out, wanting to somehow become like everyone else. If she only knew how.

She tried to focus on the one-room studio apartment that housed her spanking-new leather couch, several cockroaches and her first set of dishes. On this particular Saturday night, the chosen project was putting up a shower curtain. She didn't own a screwdriver, so tried to make do with a butter knife. She discovered that a butter knife was very good for putting holes in Sheetrock, but a poor tool for attaching a curtain rod. She was seriously considering duct taping the thing to the wall when someone knocked on her door.

She didn't know anyone in New York. She did know, however, how dangerous New York could be for a woman alone. To be on the safe side, she took her butter knife with her to answer the door. She also made a mental note to somehow install a peephole at the first opportunity, perhaps again using the all-purpose, handy-dandy butter knife.

Keeping the chain latched at the top of the door, she peered out. The hallway light had long ago burned out, so it was difficult to see. The bulky shape of a jacket, the glint of a belt buckle...and the most piercing pair of blue eyes New York had ever seen. They provided more light than a light bulb ever could.

"Holy cow," she heard herself say.

"Holy cow to you, too," Tyler replied easily. "Can I come in before I get eaten by one of these mice?"

Gladiator.

Fingers shaking, Jenny unlocked the chain and stepped back. Tyler walked in with his lazy, trademark saunter, as if he'd visited here a thousand times before. He didn't look like a New Yorker. In Jenny's limited experience, New Yorkers always looked either angry or bored. Tyler looked like something she might have dreamed up—a vivid, larger-than-life man whose presence was every bit as powerful as his absence had been. He was wearing a denim jacket over a pale-blue shirt, with stonewashed jeans and his beloved cowboy boots. His hair was longer than when she'd seen him last, curling over the collar of his jacket. His faint crooked smile, beguiled, mystified her with a heart-lifting sensuality.

"Hey, Trouble," he said softly. "Long time no see."

Jenny was in shock. She stared at him, helplessly gesturing with her screwdriver/butter knife. "You...how... what are you doing here?"

Tyler just smiled and ignored the question, looking around the small studio apartment. There was a kitchenette in the corner, the tiny counter crowded with a toaster, can opener and Crock-Pot. They all looked new. A small bed nestled against the wall, sporting a blue comforter that also looked new. Ditto the coffee table and the sofa. "Jenny, you'd better watch yourself. This looks like you might actually be *nesting* here." Then, before she could reply, "Why are you carrying around that knife?"

"I was putting up a shower curtain."

He nodded, as if she actually made sense. His eyes drifted to a magazine on a coffee table and stuck there. His smile grew wider and brighter. "So that's where it went. I wondered. You haven't forgotten me, after all."

Jenny's cheeks felt seriously sunburned. She put down her weapon and hid her shaking hands in the pockets of her baggy bib overalls. These were her Saturday-night overalls, her uniform for messy, do-it-yourself projects. She found herself wishing she was wearing something else. Anything else.

In a voice that was froggy with nerves, she said, "How did you find me?"

"Eliot said you were in New York. I did the rest." Tyler turned and faced her for the first time. Though he didn't show it, he was nervous. Still, his eyes drank her in like a starving man taking in water. Whatever happened, just seeing her again would be worth the trip. Her overalls were shapeless, her hair hanging down her back in a fat braid. She wore no makeup and needed none. Her doe eyes carried a startled quality, very bright above her flushed cheeks.

"I missed you," he said.

That threw her. Unvarnished honesty in this situation was something she hadn't expected. She opened her mouth to say something. Nothing came.

"Cat got your tongue?" Tyler asked innocently. "This isn't the outspoken Jenny Kyle I know and love."

Love. The single word was dangerous enough to kick

Jenny's speech into overdrive. "It couldn't have been easy. Finding me, I mean. This is a really big city. Can you imagine how many people live here? There's so much to see, and usually—"

"Be quiet," Tyler said gently, placing his finger over her lips. "You're going to hyperventilate. Have you missed *me*?"

Jenny blinked once, her vision misting over. She stepped back, away from his hand, away from the magnetic field the man seemed to have. This was so much to take in all at once, too much. After four weeks of nothing but Tyler's one-dimensional photo on an old magazine, here he was. Three-D and in full color.

"I've missed you," she said almost inaudibly.

Tyler raised his brows in a questioning arch. "Then why are you backing up? Wouldn't it be nice if you threw yourself in my arms and scattered kisses all over my face? Wouldn't it?"

"Tyler—"

He sighed heavily. "I have to do everything."

He crossed the floor in two steps, taking her into his arms with all the dash and confidence of Valentino himself. He'd wanted this woman desperately for four long weeks, and he wasn't about to waste any more time. His kiss was long and deep and hard, the kiss of a man who'd waited far too long already.

Jenny lifted on her toes, her hands clinging to the front of his denim jacket. He hadn't given her time to get her defenses firmly in place. She melted into him like hot wax, too bemused and shocked to do anything besides respond. Her legs were up to mischief, threatening to buckle. The questing pressure of his lips made her gasp, imparting deep, traveling sensations in her most secret parts. Rain comes when the wind calls, Jenny thought wildly. One touch and I'm gone.

He pulled back, cradling her face in his hands, staring at her flushed face with rapt attention. Her breath caught in her throat, recognizing the emotion in his glittering eyes. Then, with the slow-moving eroticism of a dream, his head bent to hers, kissing first one cheek, then the other. Another kiss on her lips, placed with exquisite care. "Jenny...you are the sweetest, most amazing—" another kiss on the pink tip of her nose "—most adorable..."

"We can't do this." Racked with a sudden shiver, Jenny pulled away from him, wrapping her arms around her body. "This won't solve it. Nothing's changed, Tyler. I still can't...you're not...I could never..."

She was thinking too much again. "Want to go out to dinner?" Tyler asked.

Her head was spinning. "What?"

"I'm really hungry," he said, sitting down on the sofa as if he had all the time in the world. "I'll read this fine copy of *American Cowboy* while you change. Or you can go in your overalls, except you have that white dust all over—"

"Sheetrock," Jenny said numbly.

"Whatever. I'll wait here."

That seemed to be the end of the conversation. Jenny was either unwilling to confront him about his plans or too befuddled. She truly didn't know which. And so, still clutching her butter knife, she went to the small closet in the corner, pulled out a skirt and top, then headed to the bathroom to change.

It didn't seem like her gladiator would take no for an answer.

* * *

They ate at a little Italian place not far from Jenny's apartment. The food was good, which was fortunate. Chewing gave Jenny something to do while Tyler carried on the conversation pretty much single-handedly. He mentioned that Rosie and Eliot were seeing one another on weekends, which was yet another shock for Jenny. No matter how hard she tried, she couldn't picture Eliot Dearbourne with Rosie and the boys. She was brash, open and funny, he was polite, particular and extremely cautious. And the twins...they were a handful in and of themselves. That just went to show that you never knew how people would react to one another. Logic didn't seem to have a say when it came to matters of the heart.

Still, now and then she caught him staring at her in a certain way, and she thought, He wants to touch me. And it amazed her how badly she wanted that touch.

After dinner they walked the six blocks back to the apartment. Jenny had herself worked up into a controlled state of panic by the time they got home. She had no idea why Tyler had come, what he wanted or where he planned on spending the night. She also had no idea what to do about her own quivering sensitivity. The fact was, throughout her Italian dinner, she had quietly lusted. She knew passion would solve nothing, that it was passion that had got her into this mess in the first place, but that didn't stop her. He was beautiful to her, and she had missed his touch more than she had ever imagined possible. Hence, the lust.

She turned on the lamp near the sofa, trying to dispel the soft, romantic shadows in the room. Turning to face Tyler, she realized she had made a mistake. The fuller light detailed his features, gilding his smile and lingering on the soft golden strands in his hair. Up close and personal, he was far more charismatic than the man on the cover of *American Cowboy* could ever be.

There was a long moment when neither of them spoke, when Tyler caught and held her in his gaze. He seemed content just to look at her, but the extended silence made Jenny squirm.

"Please don't do that," she said hoarsely. "You've been doing that all night."

"Doing what?"

"Staring at me."

"I told you," he said simply. "I missed you. Would you mind sitting down for a minute?"

"Why?"

Gently he took her arm, leading her to the sofa. "Sit. There are a thousand things I'd like to do to you tonight...right now, in fact...but instead, we'll talk."

She sat, more because her knees buckled than anything else. Her slim-fitting black linen skirt rode up to her thighs, which Tyler noticed with a put-upon sigh.

"I like the skirt even better than the overalls," he said. "But I digress. You know, this is a very bad apartment. It needs some serious repairs. Well, actually it needs a bulldozer, but we won't go there. You really have your work cut out for you."

Jenny gaped up at him, oddly disappointed. "You wanted to tell me that? That's what you wanted to talk to me about, this *apartment?*"

He shrugged. "No, but I thought it would be a good way to open up the subject of what you need and don't need. Why did you rent this place? I thought you were a gypsy."

"I am a gypsy," she muttered. "But even gypsies need to pull their wagons in a circle around the old campfire now and then."

He grinned, his smile lighting his eyes. "Oh, that's good. Prickly to the end, aren't you? There are a few drawbacks to being a gypsy. If you never put down roots, you'll always be a slave to the wind. That can get lonely."

"We gypsies are very plucky. Very independent." She stood up abruptly, the skirt sliding down to a decent hemline. "Would you like coffee?"

He gently but firmly pushed her back on the sofa, the skirt whipping up to near-centerfold height. "No, love. No coffee. No more evasions. No more running away. Tonight you're going to do something new and exciting. You're going to be normal."

"I resent that! You're implying—"

"Tonight," he went on, quelling her with one of his sheriff looks, "You're going to take advantage of your right to remain silent while I talk. Staggering, isn't it? No, no...just sit there and listen." He took a deep breath, slowly pacing the length of the sofa. "Okay. First, I want you to know I forgive you."

"For *what?*" she sputtered. Once more they repeated the stand-up, get-pushed-down-again thing.

"For leaving me," Tyler said. "For doubting us. For insisting on being alone when it isn't necessary anymore. For being scared. For making me crazy. For humiliating me in front of all those passengers on a Greyhound bus. For *giving up.*"

Jenny's nose was suspiciously pink. "I told you. I told you—"

"I know what you told me. Now I'm going to tell you something." He fished something out of the pocket of his jacket. It was a small velvet box, Jenny saw, the kind one would expect some sort of ring to hide in. Like an *engagement* ring. Her mind froze on that little blue box.

Her heart stopped. Her hands started perspiring, a deep-rooted chain reaction. Suddenly it was hunting season and Bambi was cornered.

"Tyler," she croaked, "don't you dare—"

He kicked the coffee table out of the way, going down on one knee. Then he winced, changing knees. "I forgot. Bad knee from an old rodeo injury. *Ahem*." He gave her a cherub's smile, sky-blue eyes crinkling engagingly. "I love and adore you, Jenny Maria Kyle. Yes, there it is, that four letter word—*love*. Will you do me the honor of—"

Jenny was battling for air like a swimmer heading for the surface. "Tyler! Don't you—"

"Will you shut up and let me finish?"

"No! Absolutely not! You have no idea what you're—"

He clapped his free hand over her mouth. It seemed like he was always doing that to her. Still, whatever got the job done. "Jenny, angel face, sweet cheeks, honey bun...will you please...please..."

Jenny waited, big eyed and paralyzed from the nose down.

"...*not* marry me?" Tyler asked sweetly.

She blinked. *"What?"*

"I said, will you please not marry me?"

"You don't want me to marry you?" she echoed. "Did I hear you right? You just asked me to *not* marry you?"

"That's right." He waited patiently for his answer. "Well?"

"One of us is crazy," she said. "Maybe both of us. You came all this way to ask me *not* to marry you?"

"You seem to be having trouble grasping the concept," Tyler said cheerfully. "If you don't marry me, you won't be threatened. You'll have time to get used to the idea of having me around. Whenever you get an urge to bolt, I'll bolt with you. Wherever you go, whatever you do...I want to do it with you. You and me, free as the birds, nowhere to go and all the time in the world to get there. What do you think?"

"Think?" Jenny shook her head, trying to clear the cobwebs out of her brain. "I don't know what I think. If you don't want to marry me, what's in the box?"

"I didn't say I didn't *want* to marry you," he replied patiently. "I have every intention of marrying you at some point. I just want to know my bride won't break out in nervous hives on our wedding day. That may take some time. In the meantime..." He flipped open the velvet box with his thumb, presenting it to her with a flourish.

Jenny stared at the silver key nestled in the soft blue material. An engagement ring it wasn't. "What is that?"

"Your Harley key. You left it, along with the Harley and me, back in Bride Falls on Her Head. I brought it— and me—all this way to you. Until the weather turns cold, we can play on it. After that, we'll switch to a car. If you want, of course. Everything is contingent on your approval."

"I can't believe this," she whispered. "I don't know what to say."

"That's the beauty of the scheme," he said. "You don't have to do anything different. You just have to let me tag along. My old rodeo buddies used to say I was highly entertaining when we were on the road."

"I just bet you were," Jenny said dumbly. "Tyler...you're forgetting Rosie. And the twins. And Ella. And your job—"

"That's something else I have to tell you," he said.

"I am currently unemployed. I quit my job. My deputy sheriff is filling in until the election, and enjoying it far more than I ever did. Rosie could very well end up in Los Angeles with Dearbourne. If not, she's more than capable of looking after things. She grew up while I was busy being overprotective. Can I get up and sit by you? You're too far away."

Jenny nodded in slow motion, her vision misting as she tried to take it all in. She'd just spent a month trying to figure out a way to live without him. She had resigned herself to being a wretched, miserable spinster who knew exactly what she was missing. Tyler was a tough act to follow. Impossible, in fact.

Tyler sat down beside her, putting his finger beneath her chin and turning her to face him. "Sweetheart? You're not saying much. I'll try this one more time. Will you please not marry me?"

"What about your someday house?" She was crying now, the tears rolling down her cheeks and plopping on her hands. "You can't leave that. You love it there. You wanted to get old there, that's what you said."

"And we will, Jenny. Together. But the beauty of someday houses is that they're in the future. Whenever we're ready, we can build our someday house. In the meantime, I really don't want to miss one more day with you."

She stared at him, chest heaving and her lower lip quivering. "It's so *scary*. Needing you. It's been just me for so long…"

"I know," he whispered. "I know how scary it is. I'm not asking for anything but the chance to be there for you. The rest will come. We've got all the time in the world, angel."

Jenny looked at the box still in his hand. She got a

faint, lopsided grin. "Only you would do something like this, Sheriff."

"Only you would make something like this necessary," he said. "You're quite a warrior in your own way."

"I am, aren't I?" She gave a watery giggle. "So much trouble. Tyler, are you sure you know what you're getting into? You're giving up so much—"

"I'm giving up nothing. I'm getting everything. I don't want to chain your soul, Jenny Kyle. I just want to hold your hand while we find our place in this world. I'll take you to Albuquerque and show you sunsets you've only seen in your dreams. We'll make snow angels in Aspen at Christmas. We'll laugh and we'll love and we'll live without a single regret or lost opportunity. And if you need me...I promise you I'll always be there. Always."

Jenny had never been asked *not* to marry someone before. It turned out to be a very emotional and moving experience. Without consciously making the decision, she threw herself in Tyler's arms like a whirlwind, kissing every part of his face she could reach. The tears still came, but somewhere along the way they had changed to tears of relief and joy. Suddenly, blessedly, the reasons for her isolation weren't so easy to see anymore.

Tyler was laughing and kissing her as if he weren't going to stop anytime soon. The ring box rolled off his lap and onto the weathered wooden floor. The Harley key went sliding into a crack where the floorboard was missing. "Jenny? The suspense is killing me. Is this a 'yes'?"

She pulled back, tears dripping off her chin, and the smile in her eyes said yes. "I will be happy not to marry you, Tyler Cook. And I will hold your hand wherever we go. And someday…someday I would love to help you build your ranch on the mountains above Bride Falls on Her Head. I'm very handy, you know. I wield a mean butter knife.''

When he could speak, he said, ''No hesitation?''

''None,'' she whispered, amazed that it was true. For so long she had been living with the grief of a child. With Tyler's help she had found within herself the strength of a woman.

He had a permanent tightness in his loins and his body temperature felt like it was around a hundred and four. Jenny symptoms. ''There's one thing we should take care of right away. This apartment…really needs help.''

Her smile blossomed, dazzling him. ''So did I, once upon a time. You handled that pretty well. Besides, we have to start somewhere, don't we?''

Again a kiss, hungry, anxious and shudderingly sweet. ''Now,'' he whispered. ''I think we'll start now.''

Epilogue

The someday house had four walls and a roof.

It was a good thing, as it had been storming since early that morning. Jenny and Tyler had taken shelter, sitting cross-legged in what would be the living room. Or great room, as Tyler called it. He loved the idea of a great room, a place where only good things would happen. From that point on they had called everything great—the great kitchen, the great bathroom, the great bedroom.

Jenny watched the rain dwindle, mists of low-lying vapor obscuring the little town far below them. She wore a heavy leather tool belt around her tiny waist, which Tyler thought was about the sexiest thing he had ever seen. Over the past six months he had said the same thing several times: she was sexy in Florida with zinc oxide on her nose, she was sexy in Colorado when she wore thermal underwear, and she was *overwhelmingly* sexy in a Cancun hotel room when she wore nothing but a floppy sombrero.

He was an easy man to please.

In the beginning Jenny had difficulty adjusting to simple happiness. It took her a long time to believe that she would be safe looking forward to tomorrow, and the day after tomorrow. But gradually it had happened, she and Tyler began making plans for things to come—like weddings and children.

Patience had paid off. The wedding part had been nearly a month earlier, when they came home to Bridal Veil Falls to marry. It had been Jenny, in fact, who had gone down on one knee, asking Tyler if he would rethink his decision not to marry her. That's when she saw the shimmer of tears in his eyes for the first time. Her cowboy wasn't so tough, after all.

They had married on the exact spot where their house now stood. Grady Hansen had been Tyler's best man, and Rosie Dearbourne had stood next to Jenny. Rosie's husband, Eliot, had bought three new bow ties for the occasion. One for him, and one each for the twins. And their honeymoon, true to form, had been highly unusual and very entertaining—they had traveled to North Dakota to buy prime rodeo stock. Tyler intended to supply the Pro Rodeo Association with the finest bucking horses and bulls to be found in the United States and Canada. It was a way for him to stay involved with the sport without getting personally beat up.

Remembering her initiation into the finer points of breeding prize stock, Jenny smiled. Tyler noticed, as he noticed everything about her.

"What?" he asked.

"I like my life," she said simply. She tucked her head against Tyler's shoulder, rubbing her cheek on his shirt.

"All the unexpected things...that's half the fun. Take Rosie and Eliot, for example. Who would have expected those two to get together? And Rosie being pregnant already...that just goes to show you that you can't anticipate people. You think you have them all figured out and then—wham, everything changes."

Tyler kissed the top of her head, inhaling the sweet fragrance of her hair. "Eliot and Rosie had a little wham themselves this morning. I've been meaning to tell you. They went for Rosie's ultrasound today." He paused for effect. "It's twins."

Jenny's head whipped back as she stared up at him. "You're kidding me! Twins?"

"That's what the doctor said. Of course, we're talking about Grady here, so he could be wrong. For all we know, it could be quintuplets. I still doubt Grady actually went to medical school. I think he went fishing in Alaska for four years."

"Twins," Jenny echoed again. She sputtered with laughter. "Oh, my. It's a good thing we came back here, Tyler. They're going to need help with crowd control."

Tyler smiled down at the love and light of his life. Her laughter came easily these days, and her demons had been long banished. She had become almost like a child again, seeing and learning and growing as if all for the first time. Her wounded soul had become whole. Now and then the sadness would come over her, and he understood her well enough to let her grieve. But inevitably she would find her smile again, and their life together would go on.

"You know," Tyler said suddenly, "talking about Rosie and Eliot reminds me. There's been something I've been wanting to ask you."

Jenny caught his chin in her hand, placing a soft kiss over his mouth. "Ask away."

"You know how it took you five months to marry me after I asked you *not* to marry me?"

Curiosity wrinkled her brow. "Yes?"

"I figured I'd better plan ahead this time." A pause here and a look that took Jenny's breath away. "Sweetheart, will you please *not* have my baby?"

Jenny's lips curled into a Mona Lisa smile. "Sorry. I can't do that."

Tyler raised his brows curiously. "And why not?"

"Because—" she took a moment to nuzzle the side of his face "—I'm already in a delicate condition. I think. I haven't taken a test yet, but...I'm pretty sure."

She watched his blue, blue eyes widen in shock, then curl at the edges with a slow smile that came straight from his heart. "Baby?" he whispered. "Ours? Now?"

Eyes bright as sequins, she nodded. "Yes, my love. Baby. Ours. Now. You have such a way with words."

"This calls for a celebration." Tyler felt weightless, hypnotized by the joy she brought him. He cradled her face in his shaky hands, dipping his mouth to her ear and whispering something softly.

Jenny blinked. "Here? Now? Us?"

"You have such a way with words, Jenny Cook."

And he proceeded to remind her that *he* had considerable talents of his own, when it came to close encounters of the nonverbal kind.

* * * * *

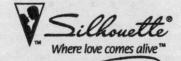

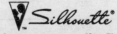

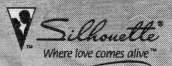

COMING NEXT MONTH

#1465 TAMING THE OUTLAW—Cindy Gerard
After six years, sexy Cutter Reno was back in town and wreaking havoc on Peg Lathrop's emotions. Peg still yearned passionately for Cutter—and he wanted to pick up where they had left off. But would he still want her once he learned her precious secret?

#1466 CINDERELLA'S CONVENIENT HUSBAND—Katherine Garbera
Dynasties: The Connellys
Lynn McCoy would do anything to keep the ranch that had been in her family for generations—even marry wealthy Seth Connelly. And when she fell in love with him, Lynn needed to convince her handsome husband they could have their very own happily-ever-after.

#1467 THE SEAL's SURPRISE BABY—Amy J. Fetzer
A trip home turned Jack Singer's life upside down because he learned that beautiful Melanie Patterson, with whom he'd spent one unforgettable night, had secretly borne him a daughter. The honor-bound Navy SEAL proposed a marriage of convenience. But Melanie refused, saying she didn't want him to feel obligated to her. Could Jack persuade her he wanted to be a *real* father...and husband?

#1468 THE ROYAL TREATMENT—Maureen Child
Crown and Glory
Determined to get an interview with the royal family, anchorwoman Jade Erickson went to the palace—and found herself trapped in an elevator in the arms of the handsomest man she'd ever seen. Jeremy Wainwright made her heart beat faster, and he was equally attracted to her, but would the flame of their unexpected passion continue to burn red-hot?

#1469 HEARTS ARE WILD—Laura Wright
Maggie Connor got more than she'd bargained for when she vowed to find the perfect woman for her very attractive male roommate. Nick Kaplan was turning out to be everything *she'd* ever wanted in a man, and she was soon yearning to keep him for herself!

#1470 SECRETS, LIES...AND PASSION—Linda Conrad
An old flame roared back to life when FBI agent Reid Sorrels returned to his hometown to track a suspect. His former fiancée, Jill Bennett, was as lovely as ever, and the electricity between them was undeniable. But they both had secrets....

SDCNM0902